<u>Cha</u>

(Saving Askara Part II)

J. M. Link

To my wonderful husband and his long hours at the kitchen sink, cleaning up my messes. "Is that sauce on the ceiling?!" Oops. Sorry, Sweets Lol XX.

Also, special thanks to Aquila Editing and my fabulously talented cover artist, Maria Spada <3

Author Preface

My Dear Readers,

This is a continuation (Part II/conclusion) of the book Saving Askara, *available in print and e-book on Amazon/Kindle; I strongly recommend you read Book One first.*

For those of you that read my Author's Note at the end of Askara, *I promised this book would be about developing more of the romance aspect between Tori and Aderus, but I feel what I should have said was: as romantic as can be expected, for aliens like the Askari. The old adage, 'To Thine Own Self Be True' kept playing in my mind, and in the end, I hope I delivered something that's a balance between romance and staying true to who these characters really are. We'll find out soon enough, I suppose Lol.*

Second! To all my boisterous but loyal cliffie-haters ;) Rest assured, I do not plan them for any of my future works. There were reasons I released Askara *that way, being my debut. But I absolutely understand your frustration and sincerely appreciate those that still left great reviews/recommendations despite it. That meant a whole heckuva lot. <3*

Thank you **so** *much everyone, for all your love and support.*

Without further ado, I give you, Chasing Earth. *Happy reading* ☺

Chapter One

Tori slowly pried her eyes open; the pain had finally stopped. *Thank Gaia.*

Something told her she'd been down a while and she felt disoriented as she looked about the room, noting the soft sounds of medical equipment nearby. This wasn't the same one she remembered. It was bigger, with a full-length glass wall, sealed alloy doors and soft lighting. She frowned, trying to push herself up, surprised by how weak she was. Why had they moved her?

Then Tori remembered and gasped, reaching up to touch her eyelids.

"Welcome back, Doctor. How do you feel? Please, don't tax yourself." The voice startled her. It wasn't one she recognized. The man stood on the other side of the glass; the brighter illumination highlighting his features.

"I'm Dr. Yin."

He looked older, dark hair graying at his temples.

"What's going on? How long have I been out?" Tori asked, struggling to sit up, her voice low and rasping.

"You've been in and out of consciousness for three days. And we're still trying to figure that out. Though, we were somewhat prepared for the scenario."

Tori closed her eyes and touched her forehead. "I don't understand. My eyes..."

"Yes, your eyes are the most telling symptom. But be assured, we're running every test imaginable. The alien covering did make things more difficult, but we were able to get you to drink, at least." Tori looked down at Henry and fingered the material. It pulsed softly back at her. The thought they hadn't been able to stick an IV scared her.

"Would someone please just tell me plainly, what's going on?" she said, growing more alarmed by the second.

As if on cue, Wells entered. "Ah, you're awake. How are you feeling?" he said brightly.

"Confused. Afraid. Annoyed. All of the above," she answered testily. "What's wrong with me?"

"We were hoping you could tell *us* that, Doctor," he sighed, staring her down. Tori blinked.

"Did you really think we wouldn't know?"

She felt her stomach drop and her fingers curled into the bedding. "I'm not sure what you're talking about."

"Oh, come now. We had you more closely monitored than any human being in history. Vid, audio. Hell, even remote viewing. If you believe in that sort of thing," he added, brow puckering.

Remote viewing. Like ESP? Then Tori realized what he said. "You had the feeds running even when you said you'd turned them off," she stated softly.

"Of course, we did."

"But that's...not right."

"This is the real world, Dr. Davis. Earth governments don't deal in chance, or courtesy, or fair play when it comes to the safety and security of our planet and its people."

His tone was flippant, as if he were dealing with a child, and it sparked some serious indignation.

"They won't be happy you've been deceiving them," she responded evenly. Thinking of the large, fierce aliens she'd been trying to befriend. She was actually more upset for Aderus and the others than for herself, she realized.

"If they don't already know then they're not nearly as advanced or intelligent as we thought they were. And I hardly think spying on your romantic tryst is cause for concern. What should concern you, however, is that you seem to have been infected with some type of alien virus."

"What?" she said, heart skipping at his words.

"We've brought in experts in genetics and virology, and as best we can tell, you've been altered on a molecular level." Tori stared at him. "Your DNA, Doctor. The changes are slight, but they're there."

Her eyes. They resembled Askari eyes...more like a cross between the two, actually. But a virus? Altered DNA? She felt her heart pick up as she struggled not to panic. What the hell had she gotten herself into?

"We need you to remain calm," she heard Yin say soothingly. "We're still analyzing data, gathering information. Which will be much easier now that you're awake."

Tori swallowed and looked down at her hands, then gingerly felt her face. Everything seemed normal, felt normal. *Try not to overreact*, she thought, fighting to calm herself...until there's cause to.

"Okay," she said, licking her lips and looking at the two of them. "I feel fine. Better than I did. The pain is gone."

"That's good," Dr. Yin replied. "It was most likely the virus asserting itself. There are no detrimental effects we've been able to detect, yet. Your eyes are really the only telling feature."

Tori fingered her lids again. Goddess, this was terrifying. Three days? Her brain immediately latched on to the one person whom her world seemed to suddenly revolve around.

***

Aderus waited at the gate to the Earth vessel, Jadar and Xaphan by his side. He had asked the healer to join him because he was the most level-headed among them. And he chose Xaphan, precisely because he was not. It had been three *sols* since they'd seen the little *khurzha*, and with each one that passed, he grew more restless.

Something had happened. The feeling was visceral.

Human attempts to explain away her absence only increased his suspicions. They said she "wasn't feeling well", asked if his kind ever got sick or "caught viruses." Then Wells approached him about giving his blood for them to study. Of course, he'd refused. But Aderus didn't like the sense he got. As if the diplomat knew something he sought to hold over him.

It had all made him irritated and peevish, and he forcibly clicked his claws as they waited for the Earthers.

The gates parted, and Aderus's sharp gold eyes locked onto the group facing them. His snout twitched. The number of human guards had increased and more wearing the coverings that Tori sometimes donned were also present.

"Representatives Aderus, Jadar," Wells said, looking at them with a smile that didn't quite touch his half-colorless orbs. The gesture was unique to humans, but Aderus could now recognize when it was genuine, and when it was not.

"Erm, Xaphan, is it?" he said, glancing toward the scarred male.

Xaphan raised his lip in a silent show of teeth, and the flesh of Wells' face grew pallid.

"If you'll follow me."

The group led them to a bright corridor inside the Earth vessel and stopped in front of a large transparent barrier. The connecting chamber was dim, so Aderus had not noticed movement at first. But when his eyes caught on a small figure, he started, ears pushing forward. Tori was turned away from them, sitting on what Earthers called a *bed*. It looked like she fiddled with something in front of her. Food or drink, he realized, as he watched her raise it to her mouth. A small feeling of relief stole over him at seeing she wore the *havat*. It would have protected her from his worst imaginings.

She looked up as more humans filed in behind them and her slight, overly expressive features came alive when she saw him. She dropped her foodthings and pushed herself up but halted when her gaze found the others, the expression dropping from her face. Aderus looked to them; he would know what had happened, he vowed.

"Aderus." Her soft mono-tone drew his gaze back. She had stepped up to the barrier and was staring up at him...

His limbs stiffened, and his nostrils puffed, even as his breathing went still.

***

Tori watched Aderus react: eyes wide, tresses flattening against his head. Yeah, that was about her same reaction, too, she thought. His apparent shock at least helping to dispel her greatest worry—that he'd knowingly infected her with something. She hadn't wanted to believe it, but the possibility needed to be ruled out. Or so said the handful of doctors and scientists that were now diligently studying "the phenomenon."

He stepped forward, making her jump when clawed fingers thumped loudly against the glass. Then he rumbled something, which is when she noticed Jadar and Xaphan. Tori slowly raised her hand opposite his, and met his gaze.

"I'm okay," she said with a small smile. "Just...shocked and a little afraid." Not to mention embarrassed. She'd just assumed that because they were so advanced, there was nothing to worry about in that capacity. Communicable diseases were extremely rare anymore. If *that's* in fact how she'd contracted it.

Her focus moved to Jadar and Xaphan as they too stepped forward, nostrils flaring as if they could smell her through the glass.

"Now that we're all reacquainted..." Wells said, interrupting them. "Ah, good," he added, looking down the corridor.

A woman with dark hair rushed up to him moments later. She was about Tori's height, shapely. "Sorry, I'm late!" she breathed, pushing a stray curl back from her face. Tori looked between them, wondering what was going on.

"This is Dr. Kemina Perez," Wells said. "She's one of our experts."

Tori stared at the pair of black-rimmed spectacles that sat atop the other woman's nose. It was seldom seen and she frowned, wondering what would necessitate them.

"Hi." The other woman waved and looked around nervously. Tori could tell it was the first time she'd interacted with the

Askari; they definitely had that effect on a person. Her gaze kept fixing on them, as if in awe, but also not daring to stare. Aderus had stepped back from the glass and was looking toward the newcomer as well.

"Em, I'll get right to the point," she continued. "She's likely not contagious. Other than potentially, blood to blood contact. We haven't detected any detrimental effects, but it's definitely not from Earth. I would...need a blood sample from the original vectors," she said, looking to Jadar and Xaphan but jumped when the scarred male hissed.

"I'm sure we can work something out," Wells interrupted smoothly. "Though, ideally, it would be the individual who likely infected her to give the sample," he added, looking meaningfully to Aderus.

"Ideally," Perez seconded. "We need to see the virus in its original environment to help us know what to expect in a human host, as well as how it might mutate or spread. Though, like I said, right now Dr. Davis is stable," she said, looking to Tori with a small smile.

Jadar said something clipped and the air grew heavy as the three of them communicated in that way unique to their kind.

"Has this ever happened before? To another species you interact with?" Tori asked through the glass, looking up at Aderus. She didn't want to force them to do anything they were uncomfortable with, and understood the type of vulnerabilities it could expose, but Tori also didn't want to die a horrible death or suffer some painful deformity. Who knew what was possible at this point.

Aderus stared down at her. "Their technologies prevented such things." Then he grew quiet, calculating.

"Your expert can gain the information she seeks aboard our vessel," he rumbled, pinning Wells with a molten look.

Wait. Did that mean what she thought it meant? Tori had honestly begun to wonder if she'd ever see the day!

Everything in her was focused on what was happening with her body, and on whatever could provide answers. But a tiny ribbon of pride still tickled her chest at his words. They were allowing another human being aboard their vessel.

The diplomat's eyes flared in triumph. "And if we still need a sample?"

He jerked when Xaphan loosed a snarled, clicking growl.

Chapter Two

Tori stood before the mirror, staring haltingly at what looked like someone else's eyes blinking back at her. They were striking, but not necessarily in a good way, considering the circumstances...

After two small meals and countless cups of water, they escorted her back to her quarters to wash and change. She had watched Aderus and the others leave, assuring him it'd be alright, but the conversation from isolation still weighed heavy on her mind.

She was shocked that her superiors had known exactly what was going on between her and the large Askari and hadn't intervened in any way. Though she couldn't say their underhanded tactics surprised her; she should have realized. Earth governments might pander to people's fears and prejudices, but they weren't as ignorant or unreasonable as they appeared. They knew having an alliance, working closely with a humanoid alien race would present its own "issues".

Witness Exhibit A, she thought. *Human female with no self-restraint practically volunteers for social experiment.*

To be honest, that wasn't what really troubled her. Tori had no regrets. It was more the way she was starting to *feel* for the rough alien, she admitted, chewing her lip. She wasn't sure how she should handle it.

Aderus's interest the second time had both thrilled and surprised her, and she'd been trying to approach whatever this was without expectation. But his reaction when she asked about 'pair bonds' had hurt a lot more than Tori anticipated, and she'd basically told him no to any future sex. Not that there weren't now bigger problems to deal with.

Some time alone with him still would have been nice, an inner voice added, right before a sound made her jump and Tori's head flew toward the door.

They were waiting.

She quickly pulled her hair back, donned Henry and met her escorts in the hall. Wells didn't want to risk anyone going back on their offer, so her superiors had pushed to board the Askari vessel as soon as possible.

She immediately saw Dr. Perez, who acknowledged her with a nod. Poor woman. It was obvious how nervous she was; the virologist was practically shaking. Tori definitely sympathized, but it had been worse for her, she'd been alone.

Their group made for the gate, and as they approached, she nearly stopped. Aderus was waiting—on the *Amendment* side. His sharp stare trained down the corridor. He never came onto the ship unless it was necessary, and her stomach flipped at the almost boy-friendly gesture. His gaze locked onto her and Tori felt the pull to him like a physical thing. The fact she sought security and assurance right then only added to the feeling, and of course her romantic brain took full advantage.

They followed Xaphan and Jadar through the main gate. Tori looked to Perez, desperate to distract herself. The curvy, dark-haired woman was the top in her field, so Tori trusted her professional judgment. Still, she felt strangely good for having been bedridden with an unknown virus that had fundamentally altered her DNA. And considering the amount of pain she'd been in, it felt eerily foreboding.

She watched the other woman's overwhelmed expression as they approached the airlock. The pulsing dark metal of the Askari vessel warmed her, but to someone unfamiliar it could be a lot to take in.

"You okay?" Tori questioned softly.

Perez nodded and swallowed. "I'm glad you're here. I don't know how you did this alone."

"Yeah, me neither," she replied, as they filed into the Decon chamber.

"Just to warn you, Dr. Perez, this is going to feel weird and intense, but it's totally safe, I promise," Tori explained. Envious she hadn't been given the same courtesy in the beginning.

"Okay," the woman said with a note of uncertainty. "And call me Mina."

"Tori," she said, with a tip of her lips.

Tori watched Mina's eyes widen as the creepy crawling sensation began and held her light brown gaze reassuringly. "Just breathe," she said, pursing her lips on an exhale and encouraging the other woman to do the same. She felt the gazes of Jadar, Xaphan and Aderus, and realized how nice it was to have another human, particularly another woman, with her around them.

Mina looked relieved when it was over.

"Do you mind if I ask, what are...?" Tori gestured to the glasses.

"Oh, I'm color-blind," she said, adjusting them absently. "These help. My parents didn't have the money for gene therapy."

"I see," Tori said, then added. "I didn't mean to pry—"

"It's okay." She waved, clearly distracted, and fell silent as they advanced. The woman's lips parted as she took in their surroundings. Tori knew the feeling, watching Mina's gaze stray to their escorts. "Would you mind if *I* asked...? Her voice was hushed as the rest of the question trailed off. It was obvious she didn't know how excellent their hearing was. "There are rumors. They say that you caught the virus from—" Her brows rose in a meaningful expression, glasses slipping down her nose, and her eyes flicked back toward Aderus.

Tori felt her cheeks flame at the implication. *Get used to it,* she thought. *It might be the first time you're being asked point blank, but it definitely won't be the last.*

It wasn't that she was embarrassed about it. In fact, she realized, she was—proud. That little old her had attracted such a fierce, unworldly creature who hadn't even acknowledged her as female in the beginning. She just didn't like knowing others would see her differently or criticize her for it. Or him. In fact, the thought of other people looking at Aderus with anything less than respect because of what they'd done downright pissed her off.

"I'm not judging you, *chica,*" Mina rushed. Tori thought she saw her gaze move to Jadar, but she'd been eyeing them all warily. The woman was direct at least. Tori liked her, she decided.

She coughed, adding quietly, "I have no regrets."

***

Aderus watched Tori and the human woman with crooked tresses and strange eye coverings, speaking softly; smiling in the way Earthers did... The little *khurzha* appeared well. It helped to ease the ire of the last few *sols*.

Truth, he was still trying to understand what happened. As far as he knew, there was no precedent, and Jadar had confirmed the same. Other species invested heavily in antimicrobial technologies, however, and it was clear Earth hadn't the need, or awareness, before.

His sharp gaze moved over her, trying to make sense of the prickling along his skin. She appeared the same but...not. It was as if his body, his very molecules could feel it. Save her eyes. He had come to accept the half-colorless orbs as human, because that was what she was. But their new coloring drew him in a decidedly different fashion. Neither human nor Askari.

The space between them shifted then and he lifted his chin to measure the air. Aderus stilled. Faint notes of Askara. Subtle traces that blended with an all-too-familiar signature...

His nostrils flared and he snorted, thinking perhaps he'd misjudged. But a second draw proved the change in her scent undeniable and shock stole over him as he struggled to comprehend it. Her smell before had not been off-putting, just different. Now? It made him yearn for the jagged cliffs of home. Others would notice, too, he thought. The idea making his tresses prickle as he realized the tension that gripped him in her absence had not fully faded.

He didn't like how Earth officials had tried to hide her away—though it'd been necessary to prevent the potential spread of disease. Aderus told himself it was because he despised the thought of human deception, but the rest was more difficult to name. There was a part of him that just hadn't liked not knowing how she fared.

A female his own kind would take insult, thinking it implied she was not capable. But Tori was different. When he did something to upset her, she let him know, but she was far from a fierce female, thrice her size. Perhaps he should embrace the urges, if they gained him preference when once again she needed, he considered. Then forced his mind elsewhere, ears dipping as he suppressed a hiss.

The reflection on little else since they'd bred was exhausting him. Her differences making his brain obsess over maintaining favor in the face of constant competition—human or otherwise. An inexplicable change in scent was far more concerning.

None of it would matter if their scans turned up something dangerous in the *virus* she'd contracted, Aderus acknowledged. A graze of guilt and trepidation gripping him as they moved through the vessel. A few stared openly at her altered eyes and he lowered his head...clicking twice to make sure none came closer.

Chapter Three

Tori stood in the middle of the same room from her first visit aboard their vessel. Aderus, Jadar and Mina a few feet away. Xaphan hovered nearby, watching. It was the first time the scarred male looked at her with anything other than apparent dislike, Tori realized.

She tried not to fidget while Mina stared in awe at Jadar's long clawed fingers interacting gracefully with a holographic display. It was nerve-wracking, waiting to know what their technology would reveal.

Her gaze sought Aderus to see his stance was rigid, claws curled. It assured her she wasn't alone.

"There!" she heard Mina exclaim, her hand shooting out at the display only to halt mere inches from it. "That, I think I recognize. It looks like what we sequenced."

Jadar stared down at the curly-haired woman. "It is native to Askari, something we all carry."

"You all carry...this is part of your genome?"

The healer *snikted* in affirmation and Mina looked to Tori with a blank face, completely ignorant of their sound bites and what they meant. Tori opened her mouth to explain, but the green-eyed male spoke first. "It's strange that it is there."

Mina's lips parted. "It doesn't recognize the virus, you mean."

Jadar emitted a different kind of click, descending in pitch and softer. "No."

Mina went still, her eyes suddenly growing big as she looked between all of them, and Tori could see her struggle to

calm herself. "We called what we found a virus, but really, I've never seen anything like it." She spoke excitedly. "Its structure is similar to an Earth virus, though, and Earth viruses operate by hijacking a host's cells and using them to produce more virus. It does that by inserting its own DNA into the cells' nucleus so that—*no importa.*" She cut off her own rambling. "The point is, they often acquire pieces of their host cells' DNA and can transmit them to other hosts, or mutate and become completely different. We just assumed it was an alien virus, but if you're saying you don't know it either..." she said, looking to Jadar.

Tori's heart sped up. She didn't like what the other woman was saying. Sure, the unknown was exciting when you weren't the person dealing with it. She caught Aderus's gaze, trying to keep her anxiety in check.

"It would mean a lot if we could study this together," Mina said boldly. "If you're comfortable," she added on a swallow at someone's low hiss. Her large brown eyes found Tori. "Your wellbeing is still our main concern. But," The other woman fidgeted. "I would definitely need a blood sample in order to—"

Xaphan snarled, cutting Mina off.

His solitary yellow orb focused on Jadar. "You and the *Khurzhev.* No *samples,*" he sneered. Flashing both rows of sharp, silvery teeth as a pair of secondary eyelids slid across the healer's green eyes.

Tori looked to Mina. "So, what you're saying is, we have no idea how I got infected with Askari genes."

The other woman frowned. "Not yet. But that is what we're going to find out."

They returned to the *Amendment*, a small group of doctors, technicians and guards waiting to greet them at the airlock.

Wells was off to the side, on a comm call... The walk back had been relatively quiet, though Tori had sensed them communicating. Mina seemed to take in as much of the alien vessel as she could, still in apparent awe, and Tori caught Jadar glance toward the dark-haired virologist at least once. She wondered how he felt about what Xaphan had said and if they would, in fact, be working together. Tori hoped so. It would be nice not to be the only human on their ship and it would take the spotlight off her and Aderus.

She tried hard not to think of whatever it was floating around in her body. Instead, Tori took a deep, calming breath and accepted it. Told herself if the universe meant her harm, so be it. But she couldn't seem to help how her gaze kept finding Aderus, censuring herself in the same breath.

Wells ended his call and approached, looking anxiously between all of them before fixing on Mina. She gave him a quick report, then the diplomat surprised her by turning and asking, "Would you and Representative Aderus like some time alone to, er, discuss things?"

Tori blinked, feeling Aderus move beside her. Well, that's what she had wanted earlier.

At the moment, however, she craved comfort and rest more, she realized. Not that she wouldn't have liked to turn to him for those things; just the thought of his inhuman strength and barely tamed wildness soothed her. That didn't feel like their current reality, though. And she definitely didn't want to do anything that would encourage or confuse him. Tori tucked a stray hair behind one ear.

"No, that's—okay. I think I'd appreciate time to just, process everything."

"Of course." Wells nodded, seemingly sympathetic.

If Aderus felt any different, the big Askari voiced no objections. She gave what felt like a half-hearted smile before starting for her quarters. A soft, rhythmic clicking almost made her stop, but Tori lowered her head and kept going...convincing herself it was for the best.

Chapter Four

"I'm sorry, I just can't get over your new peepers," Liv marveled from the vid screen.

Tori had virtually collapsed into bed as soon as she reached her quarters. You'd think she had enough sleep being comatose for three days straight, but when the adrenaline had worn off, after the scans aboard their ship, she'd been exhausted. No doubt her body was still trying to recuperate from, you know, being altered on a molecular level. She'd called Liv as soon as she woke.

"Yeah. I know," she replied, fingers brushing her temples. "I'm still not used to them either. Freaks me out every time I look in the mirror."

Thank Gaia she could talk to Liv about it. Her best friend was all she had to turn to for some much-needed reassurance right now. The details of her "condition" were still extremely hush-hush, but putting in a good word had apparently helped push Liv's request and she consequently had clearance few others did. Though Tori was sure the woman's impressive credentials had more to do with it.

"Gotta get me a pair." Her friend's lips pursed tellingly. "How did you say it happened again? Accidental contamination?"

Tori adjusted herself in her chair. Liv knew her too well, sensed something much bigger was at play, but she still wasn't allowed to disclose details, and Tori doubted Liv guessed at just how "big." "That's what I said," she replied evenly, knowing full well they were being monitored and wishing her friend were here so she could punch her in the arm. Then maybe have a good cry and turn to her for a hug.

Despite her initial reaction to what Wells said Tori understood the need for almost constant surveillance. When you were trying to protect an entire planet of people (and non-people), concessions had to be made. She just didn't like how her superiors had deliberately deceived them.

That every interaction between her and Aderus would now be tainted with the knowledge they were being studied like science experiments. Tori froze. Technically, she *was* a science experiment. The reminder started her brain down an all too familiar path since she'd regained consciousness, as she began gnawing her abused lip again.

"Don't. Stop thinking about it," Liv said from the screen, concern lighting her hazel eyes. "You can't let yourself obsess over the possibilities; it'll drive you crazy. Right now, everything is good and that's all that matters. That's reality; not the other stuff."

"You're right." Tori forced a smile. Liv always made her feel better, put things in perspective. It was pretty much what she did for a living, so it made sense she'd be good at it. When Tori had first called, her friend had been worried, too, of course, but what was there to do?

It is what it is, kid, as her dad used to say.

"And you got the sexiest pair of peepers in history from the deal, so, win-win," Liv added. Tori's resigned chuckle was interrupted by the door chime and she looked back over her shoulder.

"Jeez, they never do leave you alone, do they?" she heard Liv say disapprovingly.

"Not for very long, no." Tori sighed. It was probably one of the technicians coming to "check in." A.k.a. collect another sample. The regular poking and prodding was growing old quick, but they couldn't fit her with an insta-mod due to Henry.

"It's the vampires. I'll talk to you later," she said, turning to Liv.

"OK, love you." The screen went black as Liv disconnected and Tori pulled herself from the chair. The chime sounded again.

"Alright, alright," she grumped. "Come in!"

Tori wasn't prepared for who stood facing her when the doors parted, and sharp golden eyes found her like a punch to the gut. She hadn't bothered to check the feed, had just assumed.

"Hey," she said, a little breathless. He was alone, too. Another shocker. Well, other than the standard escorts in the background. True to form, Aderus didn't respond to her greeting; the concept was apparently foreign and pointless to them.

"Um, is everything alright? What are you doing here?"

"You are rested?" Deep dual voice rolled down her spine. Tori tried hard to ignore them.

"Yes. I just woke up not too long ago and was talking to my friend."

She watched his nostrils flare and flatten. It was several moments before Tori realized they were just standing there, with her gawking.

"Sorry. Do you want to come in, or...? *Oh*, okay then," she said, quickly stepping aside as he strode lithely into her suite. The guards gave a brief nod and retreated down the corridor.

Tori swallowed. They'd had sex—twice, for Gaia's sake. Now she was suddenly nervous over having him alone in her quarters?

But this felt different, she realized. Other than the vid feeds, they were truly alone, where before there had always been someone close by. Or the chance of being walked in on. And that Aderus had initiated it, she was stunned and...impressed?

The doors closed, and Tori turned. Her alien lover was currently—there was no other word for it—*sniffing* about the room. *Oh-kay.*

"Uh, can I get you anything? Water, or?" When he continued to ignore her, Tori huffed. "Aderus, why are you here?" It was best to be direct with them, she'd learned. And though she was confused with how he was acting, her naïve, romantic brain jumped for joy.

Suddenly, he was in front of her—she would never get over how fluidly they moved—and she wet her lips, eyes level with his chest.

"They're watching," she murmured, breath catching as she felt the heat from his body and her gaze fixed on his tresses. Tori had to fight the urge to touch them, knowing they felt like thick ropes covered in silk.

"I am aware."

His words registered, and she frowned. "They told you?"

"I sense it."

At that Tori stilled and took a step back, meeting his bright gold eyes. "Just now? Or did you sense it before, too?"

She watched them move back and forth between her new "peepers," as Liv liked to call them. He seemed fixated, she noted with satisfaction, as she waited for him to answer. Then snapped herself out of it. This was important. "Aderus, how long have you known?"

He blinked down at her with those second eyelids. "I knew always."

It was her turn to blink as a wave of disbelief hit.

"You knew? The whole time? And didn't tell me?!" she exclaimed, raising her hands to push at him. It wasn't a hard push, more just one of indignation. Of course, she forgot that was akin to foreplay for them and jerked when the large Askari crowded over her, hissing low and nudging her temple roughly with his jaw.

"No." Tori swallowed, stepping back. Even though her cursed body wanted to do just the opposite. "No," she said again, hoping that repeating it would give her strength.

He stayed close, hovering expectantly. But when she turned her head to the side and leaned away, he backed off with a snort. It occurred to her that maybe being viewed during their most intimate moments wasn't a big deal for them, as Tori looked up, noting his tresses appeared flatter.

It took the wind from her sails for a moment, but shock at his lying to her—well, withholding information, *really big* information, so, same thing—steeled her resolve.

"Just so we're clear, as long as those feeds monitor us, nothing even remotely sexual in nature is gonna happen," she said, then stated more gently. "I pushed you because I was upset, Aderus. And I know you're not to blame but you still could have told me."

Aderus stood quietly, watching with such intensity that she almost faltered.

"Is...there anything you want to say?"

"Knowing would have made it appear you were consorting with us," he answered finally. "Your governments could have questioned your loyalty."

Tori froze. *You idiot.*

Stepping back, she saw her error. *She* was approaching it from the perspective of a relationship; he was approaching it purely logically. It quickly dashed any earlier hopes she had.

"You're right. I'm sorry," she offered, and meant it. "That was really unfair of me. Uhm, was there an actual reason for your visit today, or?"

His golden eyes flicked to something behind her, as if distracted. "Jadar asks for your condition." Her brows rose slightly at that. "How are your feelings?"

Tori's lips unwillingly twisted, fighting a small smile.

"You mean, how am I feeling? Tell him I'm fine. No pain and I've noticed nothing out of the ordinary."

Aderus inclined his head and his nostrils puffed.

"Was there anything else?"

"You should be able to remove your *havat*," he said, staring at the space along her collarbone and Tori looked down. She had almost forgotten about that little issue, relieved to hear it. Don't get her wrong, she'd grown very fond of Henry, but hated not being in control.

When she raised her head again, he stood nearer. Regarding her in a way that made her lips part. It almost had her bridging the gap between them until Tori blinked, shaking her head. She had to stay firm in her decision.

Eventually Aderus broke off again with a soft, rolling click. His smoky spice teasing her nose. Their gazes met before he turned from her completely, Tori's eyes widening as she watched him move abruptly for the door.

Maybe "turning him down" was akin to rejecting his company altogether. She debated quickly, as he paused at the access just long enough for it to part. The urge to call or reach out gripped her hard but common sense stopped it.

There was simply no easy way to refuse him, she told herself. And while half of her hoped he got the message; the rest practically cheered the thought of his persistence.

Aderus left, and other than her initial outburst at the fact he'd known about the monitoring, the whole interaction had been awkward and intense, and borderline comical. But then she doubted social calls were a big part of their culture.

Tori stared numbly at the access, not sure how much time passed before she spotted her tablet on the counter to the left. It reminded her there were more pressing matters than her personal drama, and she sat scrunched in concentration a short time later—skimming briefs of what she'd missed during her sickness on the device. Tori attacked the task with gusto; anything to distract from her crappy feelings over having sent him away.

None of the Askari had actually integrated yet, she saw, which was discouraging. And transports carrying the alloy necessary to "restore" their vessel were still in transit...

Some delay couldn't be helped, but Tori frowned as she read meticulously through the reports. Things seldom moved quickly when working with one government, let alone several. If the idea made *her* restless, she could just imagine how Aderus and the others must feel: Waiting on the hulking machine that was Earth chain of command as his people and planet hovered on the brink of destruction. It only renewed her appreciation for everything the Askari went through—and continued to go through—as they tried valiantly to save their world.

She forced herself to break to eat and wash only when her neck began to bother her, and it wasn't long after that the door chimed again. It was probably the last check-in for the evening, she assumed. Activating Henry as she padded to the entrance.

"Come in!"

Tori straightened when Aderus's ethereal stare greeted her, Vepar's fiery orange one behind him. She couldn't even deny the pleasure seeing him again roused, until she noticed Aderus's stance and the aura of tension.

"Hey. Is everything okay?" she said with genuine concern, wondering why Vepar was there.

The big Askari's chin lifted. Then his posture eased as he made a low, throaty sound.

Tori jumped aside when Vepar suddenly strode into her suite; gawking at him, at a loss for words. She looked back at Aderus where he remained in the open corridor. *Oh, this definitely requires a discussion*, she thought, turning to the other Askari as he moved about her quarters with apparent purpose. But before she could open her mouth, Aderus spoke.

"Your tresses are limp. And they smell," he said in dual tones.

Tori's brows rose, having forgotten about her hair as she tamped down any initial offense. In any other circumstance, the words might have seemed teasing. "My hair is wet, and it's washed," she corrected, lifting a section to sniff. "And I'm sorry if you don't like coconut. You smell different," she added. "Yet you don't hear me pointing it out."

His irises expanded, and he drew up, making her rethink her words. But Vepar moved past them in the next instant, drawing her focus back to why the heck he'd been there in the first place.

"What was that all about? What is going on?" she finally demanded. Watching incredulously as the other Askari continued down the corridor, pointed ears rising prominently through his locks. She looked to Aderus. "You need to tell him he can't just walk into people's quarters like that. There are rules, social etique—" Tori cut off when the sound of the very air around them suddenly changed, an abrupt drop in pitch as if she'd been plunged into a pool of water. It only lasted a second or two and she shook it off with a frown, more annoyed than concerned at having been interrupted.

Though, perhaps it was a good thing. Aderus had been watching her in a way that was hungry and challenging and all too familiar. But when she looked back up to finish her sentence, he was turning away. Muscles bunching fluidly beneath the cover of his *havat*.

Tori stood staring, not really knowing what to do. What *could* she do?

"You will be at the gate?" Rumbling tones filled the corridor. He had halted, rope-like braids fanning the expanse of his back.

"Tomorrow, you mean? Well, yeah. I had planned on it," she sputtered.

An ear flicked, and he continued down the corridor.

Tori went to bed that night feeling confused and upset. The way they'd acted was beyond strange and then Aderus just walked away, without even an explanation. Which, come on, she definitely deserved! It stirred her temper but eventually she decided she'd just talk to him in the morning. Vepar too.

When it came to them, not much surprised or offended her anymore. So, the fact she felt so testy was a little odd. Maybe she was nearing that time of the month, Tori thought. Or maybe her "relationship" with Aderus (or lack thereof) was getting to her more than she'd realized.

She managed to fall asleep but woke a short time later, drenched with sweat and short of breath. Tori threw off the covers and spoke aloud to adjust the temperature in the room. Then squirmed out of her PJs and wiped the moisture from her face and neck, fingers brushing the disc of her *havat*. ...Funny how now that she knew she could remove it she didn't really feel the urge.

A sense of unease stole over her. She'd never had hot flashes before. Yet it felt like she was burning up! Tori found the bathroom and splashed some cold water on her face, leaning against the sink. A worried look stole across her reflection. This thing was clearly affecting her hormones.

She waited for the chime of the outer door, certain those watching would feel it cause for another draw, but no sound came. They probably just assumed she'd had a nightmare. Tori debated comm-ing herself but then decided not to. As a doctor, she knew it was beyond stupid, but honestly? She didn't want to know. Had already made herself sick worrying at the dreaded possibilities. And if highly advanced alien technology didn't have answers, then what was the point?

So, she wiped herself down with a cool rag and went back to bed. Sleep was elusive and fitful, the lights brightening for dawn far too soon, but she was out of bed and at the gate the next morning. On time and as promised.

Chapter Five

Aderus waited at the gate. Still on edge from his visits onto the Earth vessel, even as his sharp gaze scoured the airlock.

He had no desire to surround himself with Earthers, forced to fraternize on a ship full of them. Yet he had risked it to see her, to offer himself. A feeling of displeasure gripped him—and yes, to confirm she fared well, because he did not trust the words of her superiors. It was far from the first time he'd sought a female's attention. The difference being that Askari rarely tolerated another invading their private space. Experience so far showed it was a regular and encouraged practice for humans, and Tori hadn't challenged him—had in fact submitted and backed away for him to enter. She seemed more distressed the second time, however, so he hadn't stayed long and told Vepar to work quickly.

A slight noise made his ear twitch and Aderus refocused his attentions. Jadar stood to his right, the set of the healer's jaw indicating something troubled him. Aderus puffed his nostrils, swinging his gaze back. It wasn't the first time he'd noticed it: the male liked to quietly snap his teeth, just as Aderus clicked his claws, and he took stock, feeling them bite his palms as his mind clouded again.

It seemed his obsession with their couplings hadn't faded, and there was more Aderus could not explain. Like the way he was beginning to view Tori's most human traits with alarming interest and appeal. The near constant thoughts tested his sanity but part of him welcomed them. At least it helped curb the frustration as they waited for Earth to fulfill their promises.

His people and home yet struggling in their death throws, fighting for every breath.

Whenever he felt the leash on his patience threaten to snap, Aderus embraced the thoughts with almost violent abandon. Pondering instead on how when he looked at Tori now, he saw a desirable female—not her otherness—and a strange awareness gripped him at the idea that followed.

If there was, in truth, an Askari female in front of him, full throe in cycle and looking to attack him in favor, would he fight to breed her?

Aderus felt his tresses flatten, and claws crawl over his skin as the answer came. His mind and body seemed unshakably focused on the little *khurzh*a. On things he had only experienced with her, despite several encounters. It unnerved him, and Aderus's chest tightened as he then tried desperately to recall the last of his kind he'd been with...

It was before his capture, after many *sols* scouring the deep valleys of their home world. Seeking food and supplies, or more, a usable vessel that hadn't been claimed back into the shifting sands of Askara. He had counted himself fortunate when one such vessel glided into a cliff face high above him, and Aderus's ears had pricked at the viscous, satisfying sounds of combat as he hauled himself up the rock face.

Nothing but silence and the stench of *Maekhur* blood had greeted him, however. Along with the prone forms of two of their own. Death was a part of life, and something few of them mourned but Aderus remembered doing just that as he stared at the broken and singed bodies. Recognizing even then how precious each one had become.

She'd found him later in the night. Dropping down from the rocks above his resting ledge, obviously a survivor of the crash. A fierce, scarred female, which only attested to her strength and appeal. His mind told him these things were what attracted a male. So, why was it a human he wanted to picture attacking him? Making his *vryll* rustle in anticipation and his *pvost* shift with need?

Aderus had even let the female take his blood, the act of her tearing into his arm brief and mildly satisfying. What he experienced with Tori was distinctly different. Tempered and awkward in a way that was somehow more intense, the small taste of her blood during their last coupling haunted him still. It was when she'd been insistently mouthing his lips and jaw, her small tongue edging his teeth, as if feeding from his mouth.

They knew genuine human blood elicited certain symptoms since she had given to the *palkriv*. The idea both deterred and drew him, Aderus acknowledged. That a much weaker species possessed the unknowing means to affect them; the great forces of the universe worked often in such ways, maintaining a balance that was cunning in its subtlety.

Sound drew his attention back and Aderus blinked. The gates to the Earth vessel parted and Tori stood facing him, true to her word.

"Hey. Hi, Jadar." His eyes moved over her, measuring her appearance.

"Where's Vepar?" she asked, looking past him.

Two clicks escaped before he could stop them. Why did she seek him?

Aderus ignored the words and instead focused on the darker skin beneath her eyes and fine tresses that escaped their usual fastenings. He rumbled lowly to Jadar, drawing attention to it.

Tori's gaze had been on the *khurzhev*, but shot back to him at the deep sound and Aderus stilled. They were far below the human range of hearing, insofar as they observed. So, it gave him pause that her gaze sought him in that exact moment.

"Never mind," she breathed. "FYI, I slept horrible so I apologize in advance if I'm a bit off," she said, moving into the vessel's antechamber to claim the space between them. She stood quietly, whilst unseen energies moved over their skin.

He studied her, noting the flat rasping sound to her voice. Her head was down and she rubbed her eyes.

"Do you think you could scan me again?" she asked, something obviously troubling her.

Aderus tipped his chin, seeking potential answers in her scent. It made him recall the reactions of the others when they'd noticed the difference in it. Confusion, wariness...and a fixedness he hadn't expected. Had he not known her, bred her, would he have responded the same? He wondered. Trying to see her as they did then: A *whitz* of an Earther that looked at them with eyes belonging to neither race, and whose scent reminded them of a home each longed for...

***

It looked like she was doomed to suffer without answers, Tori thought, fighting a surge of hopelessness. At least she could say she did the responsible thing and followed up on her symptoms, explaining them to Jadar as Aderus stared from the corridor.

It was frustrating, to say the least. That the same technology that had traversed galaxies couldn't instantly tell her what was happening inside her own body. Or more, fix it. But she pushed those thoughts aside when she felt a touch of heat.

That's exactly what she did *not* need—to trigger another damn dreaded hot flash while aboard their vessel, she smarted. Standing beside them now in the corridor off the alien exam room.

Jadar was still focused on the display, while Aderus lurked slightly behind her. Tori fought the urge to look at him, afraid of where her thoughts might lead.

How she'd slept like crap last night, and yet still managed to dream of him was beyond her. Though, if she were honest, she knew... The feel of his skin against hers, the way he butted and nudged her head when excited. And of course, his very *unique* male anatomy. Which had frightened and almost repelled her at first, Tori recalled, but now she worried she'd never be the same. That her fantasies now involved roughened scale-like skin, which parted to reveal moist, pleated flesh, light gray in color, and a "penis" that sprang forth from some unknown recesses of his body like a snake slithering from its burrow. Ever-loving Reason, that image would likely *horrify* most people she knew!

But not her, nope, far from it.

Tori shifted with the knowledge, pretending to itch the sleeve of one arm beneath the cover of her scrubs. At least she no longer felt cold aboard their vessel, she thought. Forcing her focus to less dangerous territory. Henry definitely helped with that, the material's fascinating abilities never ceasing to amaze her.

He was unusually quiet today though, she noted with some concern. The periodic pulses of light and vibration oddly absent, and she couldn't help but wonder if her new symptoms were to blame.

Jadar's ears canted just then as he manipulated the display, drawing her attention and making Tori tense.

"Do you see anything? Something different from before?"

The green-eyed Askari paused, a descending click answering her before he even spoke. "No," he rumbled softly.

She tried not to let his response disappoint her, a part of her already prepared for it. But when he then began speaking to Aderus, her brows went up.

"Could you repeat that in English, please? Even another Earth language would do. I can't understand you," she said, not at all subtle this time in drawing attention to what she could see being a real problem around other humans. Not to mention that what they were talking about likely pertained to her, so she had a right to know.

Aderus hiss-rumbled a response from behind her and Tori sighed in defeat; for now.

Her attention caught on two Askari ahead of them in the corridor just then. They were some distance away but something about the way they were poised—motionless, staring—sent chills over her heated flesh. It reminded her of how a predator might watch an animal they'd not seen before. Tentative, but with interest. She wanted to tug Aderus's arm to draw attention to it, but that would require touching him: the exact thing she was trying to avoid right now so, no.

The guttural sounds of them speaking had just quieted when a feeling of general malaise gripped her. Tori frowned, an arm going to her midsection. "Do you two mind if I take a break? I'm suddenly not feeling so well," she told them, and didn't wait for a response. Instead she started off toward where her and Aderus usually broke to eat, the large room thankfully in the opposite direction of the two down the corridor.

She sensed that someone followed, probably Aderus. She hoped Aderus. Even feeling lousy and uncertain of their relationship, he was still the person she'd rather have near her over anyone else, except maybe Liv.

Tori picked out the subtle shimmer of the entrance against muted black walls, paying little mind as she walked through what had once baffled her. She immediately sat, feeling feverish and lightheaded. Maybe even a little nauseous, she gauged. Swallowing several times to try and settle her stomach. She straightened slightly; gaze still downcast...which is when she saw it.

It lasted only a moment and Tori froze, her heart skipping at the sight. Perhaps she was seeing things. But then it happened again: a wash of black contrasting the vessels of her hand like tree roots reaching across the forest floor.

Tori struggled to accept what she witnessed, as, despite feeling dizzy and flushed, her blood turned cold.

Chapter Six

Aderus carefully followed when Tori walked away after announcing she did not feel well. She appeared no different, but humans were more intolerant to changes in their bodies, he'd observed. Jadar showed interest but continued his ministrations as she made her way to where they usually ate. It was a place she'd sought often while aboard their vessel and in contrast to the glaring, encumbered Earth ship, Aderus could not blame her.

She sat curled into herself inside the space, cradling her head.

There was little about her he considered threatening. Still, his limbs tensed, and claws locked out of experience. That Earthers tolerated, even desired proximity to others when ill was unnatural, so Aderus stepped closer with vigilance. His eyes flicking over her stooped form.

"Aderus?"

Her voice sounded strange, attention focused not on her lap but on her hands. He realized, when she held them out to him. They trembled, and a sharp scent made him snort. Then Aderus blinked, watching as dark lines appeared beneath her pale flesh. The *khurzha's* head jerked up, eyes wider than he had ever seen them.

"W-What's happening?"

His muscles clenched in response to her panic while he tried to understand it. Her breaths were shallow, chest beginning to heave with the effort. He loosed a low bellow for Jadar, surprised if even she did not sense the air vibrate with it. Beyond that, he did not know how to help her.

"We need to figure out what's happening to me!"

Tori bolted from the seat, moving past him surprisingly fast. Once outside the space, however, she seemed less sure. Aderus watched as she paced the corridor, her frantic actions provoking an equally compelling response in him. His ears rose, irises narrowing to track her movements. Aderus jerked as he recognized the feeling. Had it been so long?

He had forgotten what it was to be Askari, he realized. Pain tearing through his chest. Their enemy had taken that from them, too, when they invaded their world. Exterminating most of the large prey that roamed the cliffs in an effort to starve them out. Suddenly, Aderus wanted nothing more than to tear them apart. Break through one's hard, bone-like skin to shred the soft delicate tissues beneath with teeth and claws, over and over, until—

"Where's Jadar?"

Tori's pinched mono-tone pulled him from the fantasy. She was searching for the healer and guilt lashed at him, though he couldn't name why. His tresses stiffened, feeding off her distress. Aderus hissed. But Tori surprised him again when she started down the passageway in a kind of trot, moving faster than he'd seen any human so far.

***

Tori couldn't stand still when only Goddess knew what crawled through her veins. Her heart raced with near-panic as she jogged down the corridor back toward where she'd just come. Hoping to the powers that be that if Jadar scanned her now, they would find out what was going on. The dizziness and nausea of a few moments ago was drowned out by a barrage of other things. Bad things. All the horrific possibilities of what could be happening.

She'd seen Aderus's tresses puff and something predatory transform his features right before she took off. It had been hair-raising, and Tori knew instinctually she should stop but pure adrenaline fueled her body and brain. *Find Jadar, get to the scanner*. It was all that mattered.

"Jadar?" she called out breathlessly.

Ominous clicks from behind told her Aderus followed. She knew there'd be little time before he caught up with her and she was right. A loud scraping sounded, and Tori flinched. She imagined she could *feel* the heat from his body against the back of her neck. But when heartbeats passed and nothing happened, she eased her shoulders. Turning to look back.

Aderus was there, and immediately she saw that three bodies stood between them. Her first instinct was to keep going. He could just find her after. She quickly realized that wasn't an option, however.

Two of them she recognized from before, the two she'd seen in the corridor. The third was new, but she'd spent enough time aboard their vessel that they all looked somewhat familiar. She struggled to remember names, but came up short, her focus still on the darkened veins of her hands.

Tori tensed when she noticed they stared with the same look from before; chins slightly raised. Her gaze quickly sought Aderus. His tresses were full out, making him appear huge and the way he held himself—rigid, molten eyes flashing—made her heart beat even faster. Someone clicked low and throatily. The evenly measured sounds baiting the violence Tori feared would ensue.

"Hello," she forced, hoping to diffuse the situation. "I was looking for Jadar. I'm not feeling well." No response.

One stepped toward her, and Aderus released a near-deafening hiss. Tori looked at him then. Their gazes locked, ripe with a message she didn't know how to understand. But she sure as hell felt the danger and it made her react.

Tori shot back several steps; everything fell apart. It was like a horrifying replay of the first "dispute" she'd witnessed, only worse. He was outnumbered, with none of the Askari she better knew anywhere in sight.

Aderus lunged for the one that had moved toward her, slamming them both into the wall and pinning him with his weight. The other male began clawing and thrashing, his swift movements difficult to track. Her eyes stayed glued to the scene while her mind raced, frantically weighing what she should do. A voice inside screamed at her, *do something!* As the other male broke free, swiping at Aderus with deadly aim.

Her gaze locked onto the other two. They watched on raptly, but didn't attack. That small relief helped to control her panic. *Maybe one would intervene?* She thought. But that was just her ignorant, human brain talking. Which operated according to things like reason and empathy, versus whatever madness dictated Askari culture. As it was, she watched alongside them. Trembling with a mixture of indecision and dismay. It wasn't until one flicked a light green gaze in her direction that a ribbon of real fear wound its way up her spine.

Then an explosion of movement drew everyone's attention, making her unleash a startled cry. Aderus had thrown the male back several feet, right in her direction. He scraped and scrambled along the floor, hissing and clicking, claws grasping for purchase. Tori recoiled, trying to retreat, but she wasn't fast enough. One of his limbs made contact, knocking her legs out from under her and it sent her sprawling.

What happened next seemed unreal, culminating in something almost dreamlike.

Tori was on her stomach on the floor, afraid for Aderus, and for herself. She could see her hands, veins dark and pumping with something unknown while a large body thrashed wildly next to her. Tori was sure that at any moment she'd be crushed. She covered her head, trying desperately to squirm away when someone grabbed her right calf in a crushing grip. Despite her best efforts, terror seized her and she twisted onto her back, kicking out with her free leg...

It began with a sound: a high, nearly inaudible tone, followed by a booming low pulse that stopped her cold. The painful grip gone from her leg, Tori slowly lowered her arms and opened her eyes. All three Askari were on the floor. Her lips parted as a wave of blue-green light moved soundlessly along the opposite wall.

Small movement from the one nearest her indicated they were alive, just stunned.

Then her attention was drawn down the front of her scrub top. At least Henry seemed to be alright, she blinked. Feeling warmth and a weak glow. The timing struck her, and just like that it clicked. *Henry! It was Henry!!* Tori gaped in shock and awe. He must have sensed her terror and panic and reacted.

Her *havat* had saved her. In the next instant she thought of Aderus, worry settling like a weight in her chest as she propped herself onto her elbows. She saw sleek locks rise above a prone body, his movements slow and unsure as he paused on his haunches. Relief overwhelmed her.

"Aderus." His head jerked up. Though Tori winced at how pinched her voice sounded when one of the downed males moved.

Suddenly he was there. It must have been sixty feet he'd leapt to get to her, and Tori shifted as penetrating eyes raked over her body. She felt exposed in this position. Him hovering over her, all large form and long limbs.

One ear twisted and she gasped when he grasped her shoulders, hauling her to her feet.

"We leave. Now," he growled, propelling her forward. It felt like her feet left the ground more than once as they wove quickly past the others, her head turning to look back at them.

"Are they alright?" she asked, voice jarring with hurried steps. She couldn't agree more when it came to getting the hell away but concern still tickled her gut. Then Tori watched as one began to rouse. His movements were slow and disoriented at first, but within seconds he had rolled onto his feet with deadly agility and was facing them down the corridor. The look in his eyes caused the hairs along her neck to prickle.

"Move," Aderus hissed.

He didn't have to tell her twice. Tori jerked out of his grip, taking off at a dead run. She wasn't much of a sprinter but being chased by something like the creatures behind her had a way of making even the laziest human being into an Olympic athlete. Tori turned her head to the side, a dark shadow assuring her that Aderus followed. He was faster than anything she'd ever seen, which meant he was purposely lagging, keeping himself between her and the others.

They came upon the first junction and Tori almost stumbled. Panicking when she couldn't remember the right direction. Then something hard hit her from behind, her ribs suddenly tight and feet treading air. She was back on the ground in an instant, legs pumping in the direction he'd pointed her.

Chaos is what she felt as they ran. Her body wasn't her own and no one had answers. Now this. Why were they fleeing?! What had changed? Tori knew there were risks every time she went aboard their vessel, but never had she felt so threatened. She hadn't even known what fear looked like on them, and the fact Aderus thought what was happening was deserving of it fucking terrified her.

As they came upon the next split, she saw a wave of light illuminate one passage. Acting on instinct, she took it, and kept going. Breath tore from her chest and her lungs burned. But she risked a glance back, wanting to see if the others followed. Aderus clicked at her, nostrils flaring until she faced forward again. The inhuman way his powerful legs moved burned itself into her brain as they ran, arms and legs pumping with exertion. After a few more turns they made it to the Decon chamber and Tori ground to a halt, hands braced on her thighs. Aderus's nostrils puffed and she noticed his chest rose and fell a bit quicker, but otherwise, he looked no worse for wear.

"Keep going," he ordered, stalking past her as Tori's gaze followed him to the gate. Her eyes widened.

They wouldn't attempt to follow them onto the *Amendment*, would they? Couldn't he just lock them out of the chamber? *And then what, wait it out? What if they could get in?*

She slapped her ear comm again, coughing to clear her throat. Miraculously, she had remembered to hit it while running but wasn't surprised they hadn't responded. Protocol required a verbal check. Even if she had been able to speak while running, she didn't want to relay panic until she knew without a shred of doubt that it was founded. Tori quickly requested access, rambling off the code and repeating it twice as she staved her breath to sound calm.

'Potential hostiles.' She knew she should say it, but halted. If she did, there'd be no going back. Maybe Aderus overreacted, or was misinterpreting what was going on. He hadn't even told her what that was yet, so how could she, in good conscience, make that judgment?

Chapter Seven

Aderus's gaze locked onto the access.

He hadn't understood at first, he thought back. Senses overwhelmed by the scent of her panic. And when she took off in a kind of trot, it incited his most basic instinct: the perfect combination of fear and flight. That it roused the interest of others in the passageways didn't surprise him. But then she'd stopped...something heady touching his nostrils and instantly he realized the danger.

Her scent since her sickness was a curious thing. Mostly human, but it changed. The faint wafts that reminded them all so much of home came and went, like the ever-fluid sands of Askara, and he relished those touches in the air when she was around.

This was not faint.

Aderus's ears had stooped and his nostrils splayed. He wanted to wallow in it; crush her to the ground and bury his snout against her body in an effort to feel like he was there again. Instead of some uncharted world, hoping on a race that despite appearances, probably held more power than the remainder of Askara's fighting force. At the same time, the image of pinning her, rubbing against her body, triggered his arousal almost painfully and his *vryll* had actually parted beneath his *havat*.

Aderus's focus had moved quickly to the others, snouts tipped as they sampled the air. They might not be interested in her in the way he was, but the scent coming off her embodied their home world so completely, there was no question they would advance. The thought made his whole body tighten with barely leashed violence, and Aderus had struck.

Never could he have imagined that the little Earther would wield her *havat* to emit a surge powerful enough to knock them all off their feet.

Before today he had never really seen it used because most thought it ignoble—a sign of weakness that one could not hold their own. Still, Aderus knew the skill was incredibly difficult to harness, which only impressed him more.

He hadn't remembered much. One moment he'd been kicking the male away from him; the next he was waking from the floor, disoriented. Aderus was thankful she'd been able to defend herself, but now feared what he'd given her, and by default, Earth.

And as he looked back at her, speaking urgently to the terrestrial ship, he couldn't tell whether the feeling that crept along his scalp was due to the ones he could sense coming... Or the fact he might have just realized the true potential of humans.

***

Tori had tried to sound calm, but some amount of panic must have been evident in her voice. Six armed guards met them at the gate on board the *Amendment*, and while their greetings were normal, the way they held their weapons was not. Aderus was a few feet behind her, chin down, eyes flashing. Tori's fingers twitched at her sides. The intensity he projected only added to the sense something was off. She wasn't sure what he intended from here, but her attention stayed focused on the airlock.

Since Earth had pushed for integration, all they would have to do was request access and it would likely be granted. Her eyes darted back to the guards again. She really hoped it wasn't a mistake she hadn't said those words.

"Everything okay, Doc?" One of them asked, watching them closely.

Her tense muscles relaxed a fraction, and she plastered a smile on her face. "Fine, I forgot something in my quarters," she lied. "It's kind of urgent."

They just had to get out of the line of sight. After that, Tori doubted the others would follow onto a ship, that up until now, they'd seemed to want no part of. But she didn't want to alarm the guards by rushing.

The sound of the airlock opening in the next moment sent her stomach into her chest and Tori jerked, in spite of herself. Aderus hissed, starting toward her, while the guards tensed and pointed their weapons.

"Stand down!" she ordered, holding out an arm. One of the men's eyes widened as they latched onto her hand.

Aderus clicked and flashed his teeth, his body propelling her forward. It was just some misunderstanding. This was not how relations would end between Earth and its first encounter with an intelligent extraterrestrial race.

Tori watched three Askari prowl aboard, unable to look away. The guards raised their weapons. "Stop right there!"

They seemed oblivious though; snouts raised, eyes searching. One's gaze found them before they rounded the corner and his ears pulled back.

The edge of the hall blocked her view then, a small push to the middle of her back redirecting her focus. Aderus was forcing her away, still trying to protect her. The farther they got without the sound of gunfire enabled some degree of reason to return and instead of hurrying blindly in one direction, Tori made for her quarters. Perhaps because it was one of the last places her mind had been, but also, it felt like safety, a locked door. She almost forgot Aderus followed until she staggered inside and turned to see him hovering at the threshold to her open rooms.

"Now you *don't want* a barrier between us and them? Get in here!" she breathed. He looked wild. It sent a chill down her spine.

Aderus stepped from the bright hall with a rolling click, causing the doors to close behind him. His wraithlike orbs appeared to glow in the dimmer lighting of her suite and Tori immediately activated the lock with a voice command. Hoping to get at least a few uninterrupted moments before several someones came searching, demanding explanations.

She shielded her eyes, walking a quick circle. "I don't understand, what was that all about?"

"Your scent." He growled, edging closer and Tori watched his nostrils flare.

"What do you mean, what's wrong with it?"

"You smell of home. Of Askara."

Tori stared at him. Wait a minute. She smelled like...their planet? She tried to imagine the same as she thought of Earth.

"Why do I smell like Askara?"

"If I knew I would tell you," he rumbled softly, and Tori bit her lip to keep it from trembling. She made for the kitchen on jerky legs. Given the recent hot flashes, she opted for water, pretending it was something stronger as she leaned against the counter. One look at her hand showed the dark veins spidered past her wrists now and she quickly gulped down the liquid.

The air shifted, replacing her diminishing fortitude with a powerful sense of awareness that forced her eyes over the rim of the glass. Goosebumps broke out across her skin. Had he been watching her like that the entire time? It wasn't just the look, she realized. It was the whole aura he projected.

Intense. Devouring.

Tori slowly lowered the glass, watching him trace the movement.

"What is it?" she asked shakily.

Dark lids cut off the glow from his eyes and she tensed at the sound of his claws somewhere to her right.

"Your scent," he repeated, drawing her gaze back up.

Clearly, it was affecting him too. Then her breath hitched as heat suffused her body, enough to make her sweat. When she regained focus, he was directly in front of her. Tori's eyes widened. She jerked her hands up, pressing the heels to the counter behind her and leaned back with a swallow. How could she possibly be getting turned on at a time like this? She thought, turning her head to the side.

If she didn't reciprocate, he'd eventually back off. She knew that.

The air thickened and a huff sounded above her. Then Tori gasped when he bumped the side of her head with his jaw insistently. First at her hairline, then down the side of her face and ear.

This is the last thing I need to be dealing with right now. She thought, temper sparking from frayed nerves.

A blast of sensation in the next moment left her reeling. Air whipped at her cheeks, and a loud thud shook the surfaces behind and beneath her. Tori froze, slowly lifting her head. Aderus was braced against the wall facing her, long fingers reaching back to steady himself. His eyes moved as if he too was trying to understand what just happened. Tori looked down, watching a soft glow move up her arms and then disappear beneath the sleeves of her scrubs. She could feel the warmth and energy of it: reassuring her. *Holy shit.*

It was like what had just happened aboard their ship, only this time, she recognized her own influence. She huffed incredulously, as an indescribable feeling tore through her.

Her eyes found Aderus again, thinking teasingly that it served him right. The thought died quickly, however, when he straightened. Pinning her from beneath prominent brows as they stood staring at one another.

A dark sound of promise filled the space...making her lower belly clench.

Tori jerked when the chime to the outer door suddenly went off, breaking tension so thick you could see it. The timing was too coincidental but relief flooded her as she barked at whoever it was to enter. The doors parted to reveal Wells, Yin and a small group of soldiers. Mina was with them.

Aderus's gaze flicked briefly toward them and her arms dropped. It was nearly cathartic to have that attention off of her. From what she'd read of his body, it was like he'd been sizing her up. For what purpose, Tori *thought* she'd known, but something had entered his eyes after the second energy pulse.

She didn't get the sense he was happy about it. And while the sexual tension hadn't disappeared, the way he watched her had made her uneasy.

Wells' tense brown eyes darted between the two of them and Tori turned to face them. "Is everything okay here?"

"Of course," she heard herself say.

"Glad to hear it. Perhaps you wouldn't mind explaining what the hell just happened then?" Wells replied smoothly, a hardness entering his voice.

Tori looked to Aderus. She wanted answers, too. But so far, all she knew was that she now smelled like Askara. Wells' eyes dropped to her hands and widened. "I thought they'd been seeing things. Why wasn't protocol followed?"

A couple of the others had been making to enter but stopped when they saw what he referred to. Someone gasped, and one of the soldiers retreated a step back into the corridor. Tori's lips parted. What should she say? That they *were* being chased, but don't worry because her alien leotard had twice emitted an energy pulse powerful enough to stun four large Askari? Which meant she was walking around with a very significant weapon on her body; one that Earth would no doubt want neutralized, or confiscated. Since she didn't have confidence she could control it.

"Em, that was me," a female voice spoke, breaking the silence. Tori's gaze flew to Mina. She watched the woman's hand opposite Wells clench and unclench at her side.

"Dr. Davis had mentioned something to me this morning. Obviously, it was nowhere near as progressed. The symptom was transient. I assured her it was probably fine, that we'd continue to monitor it and I cleared her to board. My prognosis, still stands," she added hesitantly, wide brown eyes meeting Tori's through the lenses of her spectacles.

Wells looked down at Mina, not fooled for a moment. "That seems doubtful and seriously makes me question your professional judgment, Dr. Perez. But if you wish to take official responsibility for this glaring breach in protocol, so be it. Until then, Dr. Davis will be confined to her quarters. No unauthorized access," he said, looking worriedly at her hands. "And get some suits!" He barked, turning to someone behind him. When the ambassador turned back, his attention shifted to Aderus.

"Representative Jadar is at the gate," Wells said, his tone much more gracious. "I urge you to please stay, however, until we get this sorted. Tensions are high at the moment, but it was quite obvious you were defending Dr. Davis." Wells paused, a pained smile transforming his features. "I'm sure this was just some simple misunderstanding."

Chapter Eight

"Do you actually want me to answer that question?" Tori asked, staring at Mina with raised brows. They were in the large chairs of the main sitting area, the look in the other woman's eyes more than sympathetic. She wore a white bio suit and nothing else—one of the braver ones.

The virologist insisted after a battery of tests that Tori was *not* contagious. But most everyone else that came close, including the guards, were in full attire. She'd been playing patient for well over an hour now, answering so many questions she'd lost count. The inky black coloring of her veins had receded, and she'd only had one minor hot flash.

"You know—"

"I know, I know," Tori interrupted. "You have to ask them, I'm just tired. Sorry. Um, yes, I'm feeling a little desperate," she said, forcing a laugh. What was the saying? Gotta laugh or you'll cry? "I think it's only natural, considering. But I'm not suicidal, I can assure you."

"Okay. Good." She nodded, tapping her tablet. "When was your last period?"

"They asked me that before. I'm not on anything and they can be irregular. It's been a while."

"Mm. Your hormone levels say you're ovulating. Or just did. That could be contributing to the hot flashes," she said, looking up.

Tori frowned. "That was actually the first thing I thought when they started. I asked Jadar for a scan as soon as I boarded but we should try again, while I still have symptoms."

Mina looked at her. "I agree, and I pushed for it, I did. But..."

Tori pursed her lips. "Protocol is protocol." She was a doctor; she understood the need for containment. But as a scientist and a patient, they were missing a vital window. Tori just wanted to know what was happening with her body.

She'd been mentally preparing for the worst, and there was no doubt that watching her veins change color was terrifying. She realized something just then, though. Any feelings of dread and doom from before were gone. She was anxious, overwhelmed. But she didn't feel like her life was in danger. It was the strangest thing.

"Things are tense right now," Mina mumbled, her gaze moving toward the main entry. "People are on edge; I heard 'damn djinn' earlier."

"What? Who?" Tori bristled. Unfortunately, there was no lack of demeaning nicknames among those that refused to accept Earth's new reality. Most of it was relegated to the surface, though. The vetting process working to prevent anyone with those inclinations from getting onto the *Amendment*. Even so, she supposed it was impossible to control people's reactions to perceived hostilities.

"One of the guards. I don't know which." Mina looked back at her tablet. "The point is, we all need to be careful. *You*, need to be careful."

Tori grew quiet, digesting what she'd said.

***

Humans called them *quarters*. Aderus could barely walk the area without ducking, turning or lifting his arms. The space was separate, connected to hers by a single barrier. Like a never-ending exercise in confinement, he thought. Silently skulking the myriad of objects that only made him yearn for the freedom to move. And this was where they wanted to contain them. It made his claws tic.

Faint sounds of her pricked his ears, and Aderus stilled. Jadar wanted to scan her again but the humans insisted on conducting their own tests, and Earth rules dictated she be confined for a period of time. It was probably best, since he didn't fully trust the others to stay away. Especially now, with what most of them had undoubtedly gathered—that it was no longer just an issue of her personal wellbeing.

The *khurzha* was a diplomat of Earth. The one, and only, human who had been working with them as closely. What if all Earthers developed her symptoms? What if it progressed, became mortal? Aderus clicked his claws, sickened by the thought. What if they were all able to control Askari technology in the way Tori could?

He wouldn't try to deny it, these things terrified him. But something told him that pushing now would be a mistake, so he listened. And waited... Attention wandering ponderously to the furthest corner in this crevice of living space. What they called the *arboretum.*

Talk of the strange environment was the only reason some had shown interest in coming aboard the Earth vessel at all, Aderus was reminded. His concerns having been firmly elsewhere that day.

He approached the access carefully. Moving to cover his face with a hiss when it opened, and light, bright and relentless stung his sensitive eyes. His ears dropped; nostrils flaring at the sensations. The air was hot—heavy with moisture, and the movement of it carried all sorts of scents. He didn't know how to describe them. They wove together in waves, overwhelming him where he stood.

Then the brutal light dimmed and Aderus blinked beneath his arm. Noting a light, dusty loam before someone spoke behind him.

"They all had that same reaction. I found setting the controls to dusk was much more preferable for you."

Aderus scented the diplomat and two others as he slowly lowered his arm... Understanding dawning as he finally glimpsed the scene.

Giant plants reached overhead, swathing what grew beneath them in soothing darkness as strange sounds teased his ears—signatures of creatures he did not know. Vegetation was everywhere. No wonder humans ate so much of it. The entire landscape, practically drowning in life. When he lifted his gaze further his breath stilled. The orange of *Kharhisshna* stretched above them, and purple, like Askara's own skies.

"If I knew it would entice more of you, we would leave it like this all the time," Wells said, sounding closer. "But our plants and animals need the daylight to survive and regulate their biology. As do we."

Aderus turned, looking down at the ambassador. Two human guards stood behind him.

"Dr. Davis will be confined to her quarters until her symptoms subside, or we can figure out more about what's going on. She said that you told her her...scent? Had changed?"

His attention shot to one of the guards. "It was changed before," Aderus rumbled.

"Before, when? After the initial quarantine? When her eyes changed?"

"Yes."

Wells frowned. "And how did it change, exactly?"

Aderus pinned him with a stare. He had decided he would try to be appeasing. Perhaps it would encourage the same from Wells and they could get Tori back onto their vessel for answers.

"Before she smelled human. Now she smells of Askara."

"Hm. And, what exactly were the others doing when they came onboard? What was their intention? Because, I have to tell you, from the perspective of my superiors it appeared hostile enough to cause significant concern."

Aderus loosed two soft clicks. "Did they attack?"

The diplomat blinked. "Well, no."

"Then it was not hostile."

"I see," he said with a half-smile. "Because it seemed like you were protecting her from something. At least from our perspective."

Movement caught his eye, and Aderus looked up to see the one guard shift his weapon. His tresses bristled. This was a game. The male thought to intimidate him, and a part of him couldn't help but respect the human for it. While the rest questioned his sense.

"I protect her every time she is aboard our vessel," he countered. "The others were curious."

Wells continued to stare at him in that annoyingly expectant way, but Aderus tried not to appear threatening. That was the way of *his* kind; he was learning it was not the best approach with humans. They tended to exert power politically, rather than physically. Gathering any information they could to justify their actions, or inaction. It was a difficult thing for him to accept. He hated it, in fact. But if Tori had taught him anything, it was that Earthers did not submit easily to the laws of nature.

"I see. I will relay that to my superiors then." The diplomat smiled tightly again. "No cause for alarm, I'm sure they'll understand. It will take a little while for worries to settle, but I'm confident in each of our abilities to work through these minor discrepancies, yes?" he said, motioning behind him. "In the meantime, I wouldn't be doing my job if I didn't tell you that one or two of you staying on the *Amendment* right now would go a long way in assuring us this was just some simple misunderstanding."

Aderus stiffened, realizing all too late the ledge he'd backed himself onto.

"At least until Dr. Davis' symptoms are addressed. It would be a great gesture of good will. Otherwise, I can't guarantee everyone will see it as we do."

***

Tori woke with a start to her comm blaring in her ear. She'd put her head down for a minute after Mina and the others left, thinking about what the virologist said, and also of Aderus. About how he'd protected her again and the look in his eyes after the second energy pulse.

Wells' bright voice filled her ear and Tori instantly tensed. The man was mercurial, to say the least. He asked how she was feeling.

"Um, better. Thank you."

"Good. Very good. I comm-ed to tell you that Representative Aderus has offered to stay aboard the *Amendment* until I can assure our superiors that none of this is cause for concern."

Tori's head was still foggy, but she couldn't have heard him right.

"I'm sorry?"

Wells kept pace as if she hadn't spoken. "I wouldn't be surprised if he stayed to the arboretum—it seems to intrigue them—but I did offer the suite connecting yours, should he like to use it."

Tori's mind reeled as she stared blindly ahead. She pictured Aderus in rooms that looked exactly like hers. Tall form and long limbs moving awkwardly about the space. Even the handful of times he came into her quarters he'd seemed fidgety, anxious to leave. She couldn't imagine him volunteering to stay aboard, no way.

"I don't understand."

A bark of laughter. "We had a very reasonable discussion. Seems we're finally beginning to understand one another. I suppose I have *you* to thank for that, Doctor. It will help take the focus off of, more pressing concerns."

Tori didn't respond, not really sure what to say. Was he expecting something specific from her?

"Davis, are you there?"

"Is there something you're asking of me?"

"Only what you've been doing. Rest; your wellbeing is still our main concern. But if you can convince him to stay, then by all means!"

Tori scowled, not liking the implication. She would never play someone like that, least of all him. She doubted she even could. Her eyes locked across the room. He was only two doors away. She grew restless, a stab of protectiveness prickling her ire as she disconnected with Wells.

Sooner or later they needed Askari to integrate, she knew that. The idea of living amongst them was as exciting as it was terrifying, but it shouldn't be as a result of coercion. Which this strongly smelled of in some way. She wanted to know if that was the case.

A pang of apprehension twisted her gut. She really should be resting, she thought, looking down at her hands. Tori blew out warily with relief—they looked normal. For now.

Before she nodded off, she'd thought about what had happened aboard their ship. The way Aderus had been acting before Wells and the others came...it made her recall things she'd noticed the past day or so with the others: piercing glances, lots of raised chins and flaring nostrils.

Tori pushed herself to her feet and shuffled to the bathroom. Maybe she should wait for a guard. Or have Mina go with her.

How disappointing, her inner she-beast chided. *Where's the defiant warrior woman that attracted such a frightening creature to begin with?*

She frowned, standing beneath a spray of lukewarm water minutes later to hopefully avoid another hot flash. It was a quick wash, the less-than-scorching water chilling her skin as her fingers brushed the disc of her *havat*.

What had happened with the covering was amazing, but she was reluctant to tell her superiors again. The fear of what they'd do with the knowledge warred with her protectiveness toward Aderus and the others and Tori froze mid-lather, her heart skipping. *Shit*. The feeds. Maybe they hadn't noticed. Or they might have seen something but didn't know what to make if it? She scrubbed her face, agitated.

There was just too much to worry about, too much she had no control over, she thought. As she stood at the door to the adjoining suite after she'd finished showering; urging herself to act. A soft vibration down her body drew her attention.

"You have my back, right, buddy?" she whispered, patting her scrub-less thigh. He seemed back to normal. Which made her wonder if perhaps the changes in her body were to blame. Who the heck knew at this point. With any luck, the semi-sentient material would at least keep her from doing anything stupid.

Tori spoke, requesting access, and wondered for the briefest moment if it would work. She didn't know why she doubted—of course, it would. That's what Earth governments wanted. Her eyes moved about the space as she leaned forward carefully. It was quiet, no sign of movement.

"Aderus?" she called, taking a step. Silence. It was almost like she expected it. A part of her unable to picture his lanky body arranged awkwardly into overstuffed sitting room chairs.

Her gaze found the door to the arboretum. That's where he'd be. Even Wells had said it.

She inhaled and made her way across the room.

The verdant scent of trees and leaves hit her nose as the doors parted and a gust lifted the hair at her temples. Tori closed her eyes briefly, imagining it was more than just the shifting of air between two spaces. Huh. She must have slept longer than she thought as she stepped into the evening light. Treading deliberately along the short path that led to the trees. Her gaze lifted, steps crunching the dirt.

"Aderus?" she called out again. Not too loudly because it didn't seem right. Like she'd be disturbing the peace of this place with her manmade racket.

Tori stopped a few feet from the tree line, scanning the rapidly darkening landscape. Again, her gaze was drawn upward, and goosebumps broke out across her skin. The sound of chirping insects and bird calls had suddenly dwindled. Tori crossed her arms.

Then she jumped as a loud crack and splitting of wood rent the air, something heavy hitting the ground next to her in almost the same instant.

"Jeezus, you scared the hell outta me!" she gasped. Seeing Aderus crouched feet from her. He rose slowly to his full height, claws of one hand scraping the dirt. Tori's lips parted. His golden eyes *actually glowed* in the encroaching darkness, while his skin blended almost completely with the shadows. Only the delicate shimmer of the *havat* outlined his shape, and Tori looked down, seeing the same on her own body.

Her eyes tracked up the large tree. "How did you—never mind," she said, answering her own question. Obviously, he'd climbed. A wave of disappointment hit. She was genuinely up-set she hadn't been able to see it: him scaling the giant trunk like she imagined they scaled the mountains of Askara.

Tori met his gaze and fidgeted, the dropping temperature adding a chill to the air. Glowing orbs locked onto her hands. "You are well?"

Tori tried hard not to shiver when the deep tones rolled down her spine.

"Um, better. Thank you," she said with a weak smile. "Though who knows how long it'll last."

She didn't want to focus on it and cleared her throat, tick-led by his concern. Especially considering the way he'd looked at her earlier, with an air of distrust. Tori hadn't liked it. Just as she didn't like the distance between them since she'd had to refuse him.

"Wells said you volunteered to stay. I came to see how you were doing, if you needed anything." She paused. "And, to check to see if we—*he* pressured you in any way. You know, like forced you to agree? That wouldn't be right if he did."

Not surprisingly, her fierce Askari didn't respond right away. She heard a sniff, or it could have been him scuffing the dirt with his foot. Either way, she spoke before he could, cu-riosity getting the better of her. "What do you think of it?" she asked. Turning her head then lifting her eyes to the canopy, barely lit now by the fading light.

Tori rubbed her arms as she looked back, and watched his eyes drop with the movement.

"Your sun is too bright. And hot," he finally rumbled. "When it sets...that is when your world shows its beauty." She blinked at the insightful words and the feeling of pleasure they evoked.

"You like it."

The large alien looked away with a rolling click and Tori smiled. "It *is* beautiful. That's actually my favorite time of the day, dusk. Some animals on Earth are nocturnal; they only come out at night. Not humans, but I've always seen the appeal," she babbled. "Is it at all like Askara?"

"In some ways," he replied cryptically.

She looked around them again. "This is just one environment. Earth has many: oceans, deserts, mountains."

His gaze shot to hers. Of course, steep cliffs and rock faces would resemble their world the most out of anything, and it made her lament that the arboretum had none of those features. "How is it different? Askara?" she prodded, hoping for an answer. Tori wanted to be able to picture it in her head. But she uncrossed her arms, feeling warmer all the sudden as she noticed his eyes moving over her face.

"What? Why are you looking at me like that?"

"Your eyes shine. Like a *dahvhrin*," he hissed softly, as if entranced.

"They do?" Tori reached to touch beneath them, a part of her growing anxious. She forced her gaze to the side and realized that, though it had grown darker, her ability to see hadn't really changed.

"My vision seems different too," she said, then looked down at her hands. "At least my hands—" But she cut off when heat bloomed across her chest and up her neck. *Not again*. She should get back to her suite, comm Mina. One thing stopped her.

"You didn't answer my question. Aderus, did you offer to stay on the *Amendment,* or did Wells force you to?" she demanded, determined to find out.

Dirt crunched as he shifted, golden eyes brightening—if that was possible. Awareness prickled along her skin. It always riled him, whenever her tone got commanding.

"Humans," he grunted. "It does not matter which words you use when what you want is the same."

Tori blinked, and her jaw hardened. "He forced you, didn't he. It matters."

The large Askari stepped toward her, even more imposing with the blanket of night settling around them.

"We need what Earth has agreed to give; I stay to get it," he said, looming over her. And she watched his snout wrinkle in the glow from his eyes. "Your leaders like games and illusions of power? I will play chess."

Tori stood awestruck, his words causing her core to clench. She'd been worried about how they'd made him stay, defensive even. But now she could see it was just the opposite. Mother Earth, it was sexy as fuck.

She swallowed hard and felt him draw up, tresses whispering as they expanded. A smooth rolling click bounced off the trees, causing her nipples to harden. This was exactly what she was afraid of, Tori thought. Her body battling her mind, and her mind losing. A pulse of blue-green light traveled down her front from Henry, bathing them both in its delicate glow.

Aderus jerked back. "You wield what I willingly gave against me. When you should not be able to use it at all," he growled.

Tori blinked up at him, catching a flash of sharp silvery teeth. So that's what she'd seen in his eyes before and she'd been right. He acted surprised, and not very pleased.

"What do you mean I shouldn't be able to? You gave it to me to protect me, didn't you?"

"And now you have means to render other Askari powerless. That you use against *me*. Twice."

Guilt assaulted her, but she stopped it cold. Whatever this thing was, it wasn't intentional and had saved her before. He just disliked that, what? She wasn't weak anymore? Didn't they *like* strong females?

"The first time, I was protecting myself. The second was an accident. I'd never intentionally use it like that. I'd never intentionally hurt any of you."

A low hiss sounded, and dirt crunched as he stepped to the side, circling her warily while his eyes flamed.

"Oh, come on," she huffed. "I've been in your corner since day one. I've lied. Risked my job, my freedom..." Tori tried not to react, but no matter how much she understood it, his lack of trust in her hurt. The feeling only grew as she ticked them off on her fingers and it made her want to jab back. "...my *life*."

She heard rumbling somewhere behind her now, the hair on the back of her neck alerting her to his presence. He was close as she turned to face him and she had to tip her head back.

"I understand where you're coming from, I do," she said, jaw hardening. "And I'm sorry if I hurt anyone. But do you know what I think the real issue is here?"

An alarm blared in her head, the sudden rising of her stomach warning her not to speak the words. But Tori held her ground, determined to get them out.

"I think you just can't handle the idea that a human can put you on your ass whenever they please."

A grated snarl and rush of heat was all she felt before Henry responded with a pulse so powerful it knocked her off her feet and onto her own rear in the dirt... She sat dazedly on the dusty path, gravel biting into her palms. What the hell just happened? Had he lunged at her? Tried to touch her? Tori didn't know. And what was more, it wasn't important.

Because the ensuing snaps and crash of Aderus being propelled back into the brush froze her with dread.

Chapter Nine

Tori scrambled forward on hands and knees then stumbled onto her feet, shoving aside the springing branches of plants that lined the path.

"Aderus? Are you okay?" she called, hearing the worry in her voice. She found him hunched at the base of a large tree in the blackness, as clearly as if it were a starless night with the brightest moon. Tori tried not to let that fact distract her as she halted in front of him, worst fears confirmed when she watched him attempt to rise with none of his usual grace. He must have hit the tree. Her brow furrowed and she moved to help without thought, but his molten eyes scorched her, and he hissed deep, crouching forward and baring his teeth.

She stopped to give him space, her training and concern overcoming any apprehension.

"Tell me what hurts," she ordered. He took one step and fell back, claws scraping the trunk. Tori clenched her fists. It took all she had to keep herself from going to him. "Aderus? Talk to me."

"*Stay back!*" he snarled, eyes gleaming at her from beneath his brow. His tresses were full out, falling forward to frame harsh angular features. He clicked low and ominously at her.

"I just want to make sure you're okay. I-I'm sorry," she said, raising her hands and her voice quivered. She thought she'd known what she was doing. Thought he'd been treating her unfairly. She was a fucking idiot. This wasn't some superhero fantasy; it was dangerous alien technology. "I didn't mean to hurt you, I swear. It just happened."

A slight sound caught her attention. He hissed again and swayed, which is when she saw he was bleeding. At least, that's what Tori assumed it was, dripping from his tresses that hung over the dirt.

"You're bleeding," she breathed then stepped forward, determined. Let him swipe at her. At this point, she probably deserved it. He looked just as frightening as the day she'd run after him after attacking him in front of the others, and any sane person would have thought it crazy to try to touch him now.

Tori didn't make it two strides. A sharp tug yanked her forward and into the tree's trunk just as she felt the heat and weight of him drive into her from behind. He snarled, and the small hairs at the base of her ponytail stirred with it. She'd been expecting something of the sort, like a cornered animal lashing out. Which is why she stayed completely still, hands grasping the uneven bark. They'd been here before.

What she didn't expect was the thick muscular leg he suddenly lodged between hers from behind, pushing hard and bringing her onto her toes with it. Tori's eyes widened and she gasped. A shot of pure lust stabbed her stomach and lower, making her core throb and skin tingle. It almost distracted her from the feel of his fingers grasping her neck, clawed tips grazing her collarbone from behind.

"Don't you dare!" she yelled as understanding dawned. He was feeling for the disc of her *havat*. Tori pushed back against him with all her strength, but he had her pretty well pinned in this position. She knew why he did it, knew intuitively that retracting Henry would deactivate the thing that had harmed him, negating that ability. And she was all for it, whatever put him at ease.

If she weren't completely freaking naked beneath!

And with him pressed up against her how he was? Tori threw her head back, trying to dislodge his hand but he released a fierce clicking growl, pressing her harder into the tree.

Cool air touched her legs, then her backside as Henry receded up her body.

"*Aderus*," she growled threateningly and froze.

Tori had to leash the impulse to reach back and hit at him because she refused to injure him anymore than he already was and knew it likely wouldn't do shit. She stood stiffly instead, the night chill biting at her stomach and shoulders, waiting with bated breath. She was pissed. And so damn aroused it was painful.

Her head dropped forward, breaths coming fast from exertion. "I'll agree to stay here like this, and not move, so you can leave and have Jadar look at you. Otherwise, you better have something for me to wear because I am *not* walking back to my suite, under live vid feed, in my birthday suit."

Tori tried hard not to react to the solid flesh wedged against her now bare pussy, the position making her clit throb and core clench helplessly. She knew she was wet; she could feel it. Thank Gaia the darkness hid her embarrassment as her cheeks flamed. Though if she were honest, most of the heat scorching her skin wasn't from that.

Aderus huffed into the back of her neck, something warm dripping onto her shoulder. Tori stiffened, remembering he was bleeding. He had to be in pain.

"It's okay," she said, voice softening. "I won't activate Henry. I'll stay here, if you promise to go to Jadar. You're hurt. You need to be looked at."

Tori jolted when his leg slipped, and it was then she felt the tremor in it, gritting her teeth. *Too stubborn for his own good,* she thought and pushed back against him again. Ignoring the soft hiss until roughened fingers at the nape of her neck suddenly changed and Tori stopped moving.

Claws grazed her scalp beneath the ponytail, pulling slightly, and she swallowed; fighting hard not to close her eyes to his touches. Then she felt a pressure...insistent against the back of her head. Her breath froze. The sensation triggered something deliciously wicked, flaming her arousal like an inferno, and as if acting on instinct she gave in with a moan. Letting the weight of his hand drop her forehead to the tree. She heard Aderus growl, right before a dark hand clawed the tree trunk mere inches from her own. Pieces of bark crumbling beneath its grip. Tori didn't even flinch. Instead her eyes slammed closed, channel flooding where it was still pressed against him. One hand slipped and she quickly braced herself with her elbows.

"Uhm, okay..." she babbled, a ribbon of angst curling its way through her. The tips of her breasts grazed the rough surface beneath her, and Tori couldn't help it; she clenched her legs around him, searching for relief. Aderus hissed, his fingers tightening as the solid weight of him pressed closer, trying to squelch her movements.

Tori forced her eyes open. He panted above her, seemingly just as affected as she was, though she worried over his injuries. The words "we can't" fought their way up her throat when she grasped desperately for sense but her lips tightened.

Why couldn't they?

Because she didn't want to get hurt. Because she needed a relationship.

Really? An inner voice replied.

She saw him nearly every day. He'd risked his life to protect her. Healed her, clothed her, given her the means to protect herself (though he wasn't too thrilled about it, but she understood that now). Gave her the best damned sex of her life, which made turning him down torture, yet she embraced some self-imposed deprivation because she was afraid.

If you want to be with someone not of Earth, then you have to let go of Earthly expectations, the voice said. Tori blinked rapidly. It made perfect sense. And she was tired of fighting.

So, she let go. Nostrils flaring when his textured fingers withdrew from her hair, pulling it loose. Tori looked down her body and reached blindly for his hand, slightly above and to the left of hers on the tree. He tensed when she clasped it, threading her fingers through his much larger ones and squeezing. Then she released him and reached behind, feeling up his thigh to his groin, half hidden against her ass. He clicked a warning and Tori smiled. She could feel the bulge of him but paused when something strange tickled the inside of her thighs. It was followed by a warm wetness against her butt cheek... He'd retracted his *havat.*

Tori's heart pounded, her fingers curling into his hip. The thick, rubber-like skin gave little beneath her groping as she tried to inch between them, seeking his uniquely beautiful anatomy. Aderus grabbed her wrist, however, yanking her hand away before she made contact, and Tori mewled in frustration. She tugged, but he trapped it to the tree, growling dually near her ear. A jolt of excitement shot down her spine, her clit throbbing with it. She braced her upper body, the breath tearing from her as her legs sat splayed over him. She could feel the stirrings of his snake-like appendage against the soft flesh of her behind, the insistent movements of it within his body. Tori started to tremble.

"*Goddess*," she whispered pleadingly, and felt another gush between her legs. It was like she was possessed by pure lust. Her cheek grazed her bicep, scorching in its feel.

Tori jolted when they suddenly dropped a few feet, her knees bending with it. Slaps and scraping made her look up. Aderus had dug his claws into the trunk, long arms stretched taut, holding his weight. Make that *their* weight, she realized, concern for him fighting through her very singular thoughts. His kind was incredibly strong and healed like nothing she'd ever seen, but he was still injured.

"Aderus? Maybe we should—" She inhaled sharply when his *pvost* slipped between her cheeks with an uneven rumble. All other thought left her. Even though she knew it was him, that he controlled it just like she controlled her fingers and toes, it was hard not to think of it as a separate entity. As if it had a mind of its own. Her eyes widened as it burrowed between them. How had she not noticed the strength of it before?

"Not there! Down!" She stiffened, clenching her buttocks, while another part of her actually cheered it on. Tori canted her hips, not really able to do much else with him up on her as he was. Cool air kissed hot slippery flesh and her legs spasmed as she cried out. The position put pressure right on the most sensitive part of her and she nearly orgasmed.

It was all so intense. Aderus's rough breaths behind her. His rasping snarl when the tapered tip of him found her and surged inside, stretching so fast she felt a sharp pinch. Tori's hands shot up his forearms and her head dropped helplessly as air fought its way from her lungs; overwhelmed by the feeling of fullness. She latched on and gripped hard, desperate to touch any part of him. His face pushed between her neck and shoulder as his *pvost* surged into her, no rhyme or rhythm to its movements. The initial thick invasion was followed by three quick thrusts, then it stayed there, undulating inside her. Caressing an area that, even as a medical professional, she had doubted existed. Combined with the pressure on her clit from the tilt of her hips, she was surprised she lasted all of thirty seconds.

The sound that tore from her throat didn't sound human as her entire body went rigid with release, then started shaking. It bounced off the trees, echoing through the forest around them. Her pussy gripped him so hard it nearly hurt *her*, and Aderus jolted against her back, a quick succession of clicks triggering alarm. But there was nothing she could do, lost as she was to the throes of her climax.

A grating hiss by her ear nearly deafened her. All Tori felt was her arm being jerked down and his large hand blanket the side of her head. Then, a stinging burn in the fleshy area at base of her neck.

Tori's heart fluttered; muscles still locked as waves of pleasure tore her apart. Her stomach contracted with the force of them. He filled and stretched her, the whole of him held captive by her body. Inside, though, her mind reeled. It couldn't wrap itself around what it was she was feeling. Until a low purring hum filled the space between them, the vibrations tickling down her front and teasing her nipples. That's when she knew. The only time she'd ever heard them make that sound was her and Aderus's first time having sex, and when the light-skinned one...drank. Fear quickly took hold.

Giving them blood was one thing, but this... Wetness kissed her cheek. He was hurt, bleeding. And nothing from a med bag would likely do any good. If she wanted to help him, this was actually the best way. The pain wasn't half as bad as she'd thought it'd be, which just affirmed how razor sharp their teeth were and also how gentle he was being. He could easily rip her throat out, she knew that. The thought helped calm her as the last of her climax wracked her body and Tori felt like she could finally breathe again.

No sooner had her inner muscles eased, however, than one of his arms tore from beneath her grip and wrapped tightly across her chest. A harsh growl made her skin prickle. She was completely lax against him, but a thrill of excitement still curled her belly when the blunted spines along his forearm brushed her breasts. And because she knew what was coming.

His *pvost* tore from her then surged back in, as if it couldn't get enough of itself inside her. His thigh still supported most of her weight where it braced the back of one leg, holding it bent while the toes of her other touched the ground. Tori bit her lip, whimpering at the intensity with how sensitive she was. Honestly, she didn't think she could take another orgasm.

His movements grew more forceful and she reached her free hand back, trying to soothe him. His hips were pressed firmly against her, moist folds bathing her backside, but things were so tight down there he was having a hard time moving and the sensation of it was almost too much. Tori knew he had to be close, could feel the tremor in the muscles around her. So, she reached between her legs and fondled him, framing his *pvost* where it stretched her with her fingers, and further to caress his delicate folds.

Tori cried out when his teeth sank deeper and they slid the rest of the way to the ground. She used her hands to keep herself from being squished to the tree when Aderus shoved against her, rasping fitfully. He came with hard pulses, his part writhing languidly within her. Her clit still throbbed, inner muscles twitching from her release, and the way it stroked her swollen flesh almost pushed her over the edge again—if it weren't for the pain. That second bite freaking hurt. Tori reached up, slap-tapping his jaw as air gusted from his nostrils.

"Let go," she winced, voice croaky and breathless. He did, and her shoulders eased with relief. Until he scoured the wound with a bristled tongue. "Ow!" she yelped and threw her hand back, smacking him near his eye. Tori froze, but he just clicked twice and pulled her back against him. She let him, closing her eyes as she felt their hearts beat—his a very different rhythm from her own. They were still connected, and he seemed a bit unsteady. If she had any wits left, she'd be concerned, but as it was she had no energy for thinking, or moving. Her eyes drooped to his infrequent hums, reminiscent of the constant buzz of insects in the background, but deeper.

"*Oh!*" she exclaimed when they suddenly toppled to the side. The pressure and pull of him leaving her body preceding a hot gush down her thighs. Tori struggled with his heavy arms and turned, gaze roving over him. Aderus was on his side, seemingly passed out.

Her brow knitted with worry. "Hey," she said gently, pushing gracelessly to her knees, and leaned forward, cupping the sharp angles of his face. She'd never seen him so vulnerable.

Even injured and bleeding he'd struggled to appear strong. "Aderus? Wake up," she ordered, tapping lightly on his cheek. "Are you okay?"

No response. His chest rose and fell with his breath; he seemed to be sleeping. Tori looked over him again, searching for injuries but could find none. She sat back on her heels. This didn't feel normal. She couldn't imagine him falling into such an abrupt and deep sleep that not even touching would wake him. They were too keen, too instinctual.

It was like he was drugged, she thought, lifting her hand from his face and placing it lightly on his arm.

Tori frowned, trying to think. The only thing that was different in what they'd done was the biting. She didn't remember any of the others being affected this way though. *Except the red-eyed one with pale skin,* she recalled, and halted.

He'd acted hauntingly similar when she'd helped him but Tori had just assumed it was the lack of blood, his severe injuries. And they hadn't allowed her to stay long to observe him. Was this why? Because real human blood had this effect? She crossed her arms, skin pebbling with the cool night air. When Aderus touched her, he was like a furnace, but without that heat it was far too chilly. Tori wiped away as much as she could from between her legs then activated Henry, warmth flowing down her body.

The sound of an animal rustling nearby gave her pause and she tensed, looking into the trees. An insistent glow from Henry lit the darkness.

"Don't even think about it," she bit out. Concern softening her expression when she stared at Aderus. "You've caused enough trouble tonight," she murmured.

No way would she leave him, vulnerable and virtually unconscious for who knew how long. Even if *there was* nothing to fear in the preserve, what if Wells came searching, or one of the guards? Maybe the one Mina had heard? Tori didn't trust it and seeing him this way made her protective. A bittersweet pain poked her chest. Maybe more than protective.

She scooted down slowly, lids drooping with the decision, and strained to lift his heavy arms so she could slip beneath them. He wasn't awake to fight or pull away; no long-winded explanations. Just the enjoyment of sleeping next to another person.

Tori stifled a yawn as she curled up close to his chest, feeling carefully for his *havat,* but it didn't respond. Considering the cooler temperatures aboard their ship, she doubted he was in any danger of freezing. The sight of his dark limbs covered in moonlight, however, had her trying to keep her eyes open.

Instead, she patted Henry clumsily. "I know you were just trying to look out for me," she murmured, reassured by a gentle vibration.

Then Tori's eyes fell closed, as sleep chased and eventually caught her.

Chapter Ten

Aderus awoke with a start, surrounded by a comforting darkness. His snout twitched with scents mostly unknown, but he quickly tensed at the feel of something touching his arms and chest. He reacted without thought, tearing away from it and rolling into a crouch before his eyes sprung open. He struggled for the briefest moment for balance; it took moments more for the confusion to clear from his mind.

Tori lay motionless in the loam, delicate limbs twitching. One hand was stretched, like she was reaching for something... Him, he realized. Looking at where he'd lain. Discomfort spilled over him, tresses bristling with it, which triggered a dull ache. There was a distinct taste in his mouth, and the memory of sinking his teeth into her too-soft flesh flashed in his mind.

Aderus's ears drew back.

He had treated her like a female his own kind, taking to help satisfy his needs. Though the cause had ultimately been his own doing.

Her fluid-like tresses covered the area and he pushed forward slowly, the fingers of one hand splaying to brace his weight. A swell of light moved down her body when he made to touch them and Aderus stopped, lip lifting to sneer defiantly at the material.

Her *havat* had imprinted in a way that reminded him of human traits and behaviors.

He pressed cautiously again, seeking her neck, but her skin was mostly sheathed. It almost glowed in the darkness, contrasting lines of the covering easily visible, and Aderus straightened, hoping he had known enough through the pain and lust he remembered gripping him to show restraint.

Memories assaulted him—tastes, touches, smells—and his *pvost* twitched tellingly inside his body. He hadn't intended to breed again, hadn't even offered or displayed for her. But that was where things led when he scented her excitement and glimpsed her nearly translucent skin. The bizarre beauty of it calling to him. Aderus saw his hand in her tresses, then her head dropping forward, and stilled.

He'd done it because a piece of him craved the acceptance, as if unable to help himself. An affirmation of her unwavering interest and Tori hadn't fought him. Between it and her blood, they shared the most intimate acts of his kind.

He sat silently, absorbing the truth and weight, and shock of it.

Aderus's eyes flicked back to her arm, reaching toward him across the ground. She'd been touching him, pressed against him, and he hadn't even been aware. Didn't remember anything, save releasing inside her soft, tight confines. Licking at wells of ory-sweet cruor around his teeth and feeling...fevered.

It shouldn't have surprised him. Yet, he'd been unprepared. The only one of them who had any knowledge was the *palkriv* and Aderus was loath to share the same space as that male, let alone attempt to speak of experiences. He huffed, looking away as his ears pricked to the sound of something moving nearby. When he turned back, Tori still lay motionless on the ground, slow measured breaths indicating she was deep in slumber. And that she hadn't woken when he'd torn away. He couldn't understand it, the sense of security she must feel; that all Earthers must know, to rest next to one another. Like prey animals, grouping together for protection, he thought.

Her fingers moved and Aderus watched them curl against the hard sand then grasp at his lightly. Soft skin sliding over his claws. As senseless as it was, she was oblivious, and he was loath to leave her in such a state, he realized. Until another faint pulse from her *havat* reflected down his body and he was reminded of its single advantage should anything come close with the intent to do harm.

More faint sounds and movement drew his focus again and his chin lifted, scenting the air.

Aderus craved sustenance. He had tried food from their generators earlier but every bite had been disgusting. The exotic musks of various terrestrial creatures, however, were slightly more appealing. And the vantage the large Earth plants provided meant he could check on her easily.

He wouldn't go far, he decided.

***

Tori blinked her eyes open to the scarce twilight of morning. Her head throbbed a bit and she could definitely still sleep. But when she saw Aderus wasn't next to her, a shot of apprehension shattered the foggy stupor. She winced in pain, lifting her head from the hard ground. Her left shoulder felt swollen and sore but she pushed past it, sitting up to look around. Tori saw marks in the ground next to her; he must have been there at least part of the night. She winced again, reaching up, and pushed to her feet with a hand to her shoulder.

The urge to call out gripped her, but she quickly thought better of it. If there was anyone about, she didn't want to draw attention in her current state. He was obviously well enough to move. And the way he'd dropped from above her last night, seemingly out of nowhere? It was as if the dense forest was *his* natural habitat, not hers.

She walked the area, gaze lifting to the canopy more than once. Faint light suffused the tree tops, but below was still quite dark and a short search proved fruitless. So, Tori returned to the path. Maybe he was in the rooms. He might have been hungry and there was food there. She grimaced. That might be too generous; labeling their failed attempts at *rukhhal* as edible. It was a problem, one she'd intended to address the last time aboard their vessel. But then everything had gone to shit—kind of like Earth's version of alien cuisine.

Tori made her way back. With what he'd taken from her, Aderus should be fine, she told herself. The doors parted and she stepped cautiously into empty rooms. She let her hand drop from her shoulder, not wanting to invite an explanation.

"Hello?"

Tori looked around, but couldn't sense anyone's presence and seconds ticked by as she thought of what to do. She was dusty, dirty. It was probably best she cleaned up before someone came. Especially if Aderus was still aboard, she doubted they'd leave them alone for long.

The constant knowledge of being watched added to her angst. She wondered how much they'd seen, if surveillance in the arboretum was as pervasive as the rest of the ship.

Tori decided right then and there she was going to have a talk with Wells. This was ridiculous: they deserved *some* privacy.

She paused at the threshold to her rooms, chewing her lip. It took but a moment to make the decision, and she issued a verbal command to keep the access open. If Aderus was still on the *Amendment*, the arboretum was likely where he'd be, and she wanted to know he was okay.

Tori dialed a quick breakfast and took it with her into the bathroom. She watched Henry retract up her body in the mirror, turning so she could inspect her shoulder. It was red, starting to bruise and felt a little tight but looked much better than she'd expected. Her lips parted as she gently felt the area, noting only one set of bite marks. There were secondary pinpricks from his other teeth above each puncture, which meant he hadn't bitten very hard.

Tori swallowed, unsure what to think.

On the one hand, she'd wanted to help him and was satisfied with the knowledge that's what she'd done. On the other, biting hurt! She'd bear the pain happily, though, if she knew it meant something...

A determined sigh escaped her. It'd be enough just to see him healed, she conceded.

Tori finished cleaning up and headed back out to the kitchen, donning her *havat* to hide her shoulder. A noise made her stop. It sounded like it came from the other suite. She changed direction, creeping carefully to the open door.

Gold eyes met her own, making her heart skip. She was somewhat anxious to see him after what they'd done. She hadn't meant for it to happen, didn't regret anything, but each experience with him seemed more intense than the last. A familiar sickly-sweet tang hit her nose though, and she straightened.

"Why do I smell—" she cut off, spotting something on one of his fingers. "What is that?"

Then she gasped, hands lifting to cover her mouth. It was a tuft of fur.

Tori instinctually grabbed her shoulder, words failing her as she imagined Aderus ripping chunks from some unfortunate animal with his teeth while it struggled, yearning for death. Scolding seemed inappropriate. Hadn't she just been thinking how inadequate the new printers were? He'd merely found another solution. Were their roles reversed, Tori would probably have done the same. Except she doubted she had the necessary skills.

Aderus huffed, eyes wild but focused. "I had meant to mention that the printers need work," she said, swallowing.

He didn't seem to be listening, however. Instead his attention was on her hand where it held her shoulder. Tori let go. He clicked softly, stepping toward her.

"It's fine. You were bleeding," she said. Then paused, searching his gaze. She hadn't expected to have this conversation so soon, but. "Is that...all it was to you?"

His irises brightened, and she watched dark fingers coil languorously at his sides. "It means much for Askari," he purred, and the tightness in Tori's chest eased. "You honor me, and I am in your debt."

"Oh." The words caused her cheeks to pinken.

"It worried me after. I didn't want to leave you," she explained. Hunting for answers but also trying to choose her words carefully in case anyone listened. "The same happened to the light-skinned male I helped, didn't it?"

"Yes." A light hiss reminded her he wasn't comfortable. Between this new knowledge and Henry, she could understand why they might feel threatened. Her gaze softened.

'It's okay, it's good that I know,' she was just about to say when Aderus suddenly started for her.

Roughened fingers engulfed her own from behind, lifting them easily away from her shoulder as Tori jerked, turning to look back at him.

His ears were erect, attention on the main door. The smell of stale blood assaulted her, and it wrinkled her nose just as the entry chime went off.

Her heart jumped; he'd heard them coming. "Come in," she called. The second word wavering with the graze of his claws on her *havat* as he stepped to her side.

Mina and Wells faced them. The ambassador's face broke into an easy grin. "Dr. Davis, good morning. It's good to see you looking well. I trust you had a good evening?" he said, looking to Aderus. Tori shifted, ignoring the comment, and greeted them with a tight smile.

"We have good news," Wells said, stepping inside. "I've already spoken with Representative Jadar, but you'll be happy to know, we just received comms from MAB and the *Elicitor* will be arriving shortly with the alloys you requested."

Finally! Tori thought. Gaze darting to Aderus as she watched his entire mien change, the air growing heavy with it.

"When?" he rasped.

"Ah, I believe within the hour," Wells answered quickly, his expression souring. "I-I'm sorry, but what is that smell?" The room fell quiet.

"Aderus was, uh, forced to feed himself," Tori explained calmly.

It took a minute, but the diplomat's look of confusion cleared. "He... Ohh. That's—" He cut off abruptly, looking back at Aderus. "That is to say, it's certainly understandable. Whatever makes your staying on the *Amendment* more, palatable." Wells back-pedaled. "Wouldn't you like to, erm, clean up though?" he asked with barely concealed revulsion.

Tori stepped forward. "I'll show you the sink."

Aderus's gaze dropped, almost annoyedly. Then they all watched something shoot down his fingers and back up as someone gasped. Just like that, his claws were clean. The *havat* apparently having absorbed the organic matter like it absorbed heat for energy and Tori's jaw slackened. It explained a lot. Like how she never seemed to break much of a sweat with Henry, and how she'd woken up this morning feeling relatively dry beneath the covering despite their copious escapades. He'd also commanded it at will, fingers nowhere near the hidden disc at his neck.

Tori raised her gaze, but his attention was firmly elsewhere—the transport, most likely. She knew it was important, what they'd been waiting for to repair their ship. Then cursed the fact she was still under confinement, disappointment darkening her mood. She wanted to be with him as things unfolded.

Aderus strode forward, forcing Wells aside. "Where are you going?" The ambassador stumbled; eyes wide as he half followed into the corridor. Two soldiers straightened, adjusting their weapons.

Aderus turned, glinting gaze directed not at Wells but at her. Tori stared back, feeling the emotion rolling off him. "To prepare," he rumbled. The harsh sound ending with two short clicks. Then he stalked out of sight.

Chapter Eleven

Aderus coursed quickly through the passageways of their vessel; blood roaring, senses sharp. Persistent thrums from his *havat* while on the human ship had alerted him but he wouldn't believe until he saw it for himself. Hope was still a fragile thing.

The others were scarce, those he did spot heading in the same direction. None that he recognized from before, else he would have been tempted to lash out. But the knowledge they would soon have what they'd been waiting for redirected his focus and he didn't stop until he reached the hold.

Aderus spotted Jadar, Krim and the rest. Then locked onto the tall pillars that lined the walls directly ahead. They resonated rhythmically, as if aware of what was coming; lighting the whole space with a persistent glow.

"Where is she?" The *khurzhev* soon asked from beside him, and Aderus bristled.

"On the Earth ship. They keep her for observation."

The green-eyed healer rumbled softly. "...You should know many feel threatened."

Aderus met his stare, knowing he was talking about how she wielded the *havat*. He understood their fears, had been on the receiving end more than any of them and cursed the potential it unlocked. But if what the diplomat said was true the scales were about to tip heavily in their favor. Aderus planned to keep close watch on her, and they would not bestow the technology on any other human until they were sure of the consequences.

"That will change, once they bring what we need," he said. Attention fixing on the others as the energy of expectation made some snappish.

"If still they do not like it, then perhaps they should not provoke her," he added darkly. Remembering the way a few had attacked and grabbed at her, despite his attempts to keep them at bay.

Were Tori Askari they would be rowing for her notice. Instead they harbored hostility and distrust. Aderus understood those feelings as much as any of them, but hearing it from another made him yearn for the satisfaction of watching her knock them to the ground again. A female he only just now accepted, slightly intimidated him. There could be no greater allure. She didn't even know the strength she possessed and had injured him without intent. Then willingly fed him, bred him and healed his injuries.

Arousal prickled his spines as he imagined what she'd be capable of if she were ever to try.

"Prudence is wiser," the healer responded and Aderus stilled. Aware of the male's sniffing as his ears pulled at how much it sounded like something their new *allies* would say. "Your scent—"

"I hunted," he told him.

"You hunted the Earthscape?" Jadar's verdant eyes brightened, and Aderus *snikted*.

It was surprising how quickly the strangeness of the terrain had faded, he thought. The stems of large Earth plants reminding him of sheer cliff faces—albeit fleshier—with their fine cracks and crevices. Though it was awkward learning to climb and traverse them at first, he couldn't remember the last time he'd felt as alive.

Those that ventured onto the human ship to experience it didn't stay long, just like none had chosen to integrate. But Aderus sensed a shift coming. If what the Earthers said was true and their vessel was restored, it would unleash an irrepressible boldness. And if there was one thing his people missed more, or at least as much as their home world, it was the primal drive to stalk, chase and kill their food.

The rhythmic pulses ceased suddenly and he stiffened as Jadar's keen gaze moved to the pillars. It was silent, a tension pervading the space that was nearly unbearable...until someone began to *krhune*. The low purr was startling at first, but soon more joined in: hissing, clicking, trills and growls. The air literally vibrating with the emotion of one gratifying truth.

Earth had honored their promise. And in the same act, unleashed a force they couldn't possibly fathom.

***

Tori approached Wells, determined to address the surveillance issue in her personal quarters. It had taken her a minute or two to catch her bearings after Aderus left, and unfortunately that cost her. The ambassador was already on his comm, like he hadn't missed a beat.

"Sorry to interrupt, Ambassador, but I need to speak with you."

Tori met the man's light brown eyes. "Excuse me one moment," he murmured to the call. "Of course, Doctor. What is it?"

"I want the surveillance in my private quarters gone," she said boldly, beyond the point of being tactful.

The diplomat stared at her for a moment, a muscle near his eye spasming. "I apologize, let me call you right back," he said in a deceptively smooth voice. She was prepared for a fight but was hoping it wouldn't come to that.

"I might have understood it in the beginning, but I feel I deserve a certain measure of trust and privacy, don't you? Plus, is this really how you want to conduct things? Inviting them to integrate just to be spied upon? I mean, shouldn't we have *some* integrity?"

Wells appeared thoughtful. "Trust, yes. There's actually something I've been meaning to discuss with you as well. Two energy surges were detected in the last 72 hours. One originating in your quarters and a second, much stronger surge in the arboretum."

Tori's stomach dropped. She tried to think quickly of what she should say. As if aware of the conversation, Henry loosed a small pulse, the gentle vibration tickling her torso. Wells' gaze dropped, and she reflexively crossed her arms.

"Yes, that was the covering," she finally answered, clearing her throat. There was no point in lying, they'd likely analyzed the feeds. "I didn't know if it had to do with the symptoms I was experiencing or not, and none of our equipment can examine it. I was trying to see if I could recreate it before I said anything."

The man's eyes flared. "Surges like that can be weaponized. If we could harness such an ability, it might be the most effective line of defense we have in close combat."

Tori instantly tensed. "What do you mean?" She eyed him warily, prepared to believe the worst. But a steadfastness she hadn't seen crossed his features and Wells regarded her quietly for a moment.

"I realize you may not think the best of me, Dr. Davis, but when Earth governments offered our aid, we meant it. Whatever beings the Askari are battling are even more formidable than they are. And assuming they mean to take an alliance with Earth seriously, we will still be the weakest and most vulnerable species in this fight. With, what I'd argue, the most to lose. It would be wise for you to remember that."

An unsettling combination of hot and cold flowed over her skin as Tori realized she may have been too harsh in her judgements of him. Because what he'd just said definitely put things in an entirely different perspective.

"I understand," she replied, feeling a measure of respect for the man.

The ambassador looked at her carefully, then gave a brief nod.

"I would still like the feeds gone though," she said, with as much gracious insistence as she could. "Both in my quarters and the connecting suite."

Wells looked thoughtful. "I think that's a reasonable request. You keep looking for a way to control that thing and we'll turn off the feeds in your rooms."

"And the other suite?" she pressed as he began to turn from her, already distracted by another comm call.

He quickly covered one ear. "The other feeds were never on. It was a condition of Representative Aderus staying. He had the other one, Vepar, check the rooms."

Tori stepped back, watching him walk into the corridor, and the night Vepar barged into her rooms crashed clearly through her mind.

"You know, in the beginning I thought he was harmless and the others were scary..." Mina mumbled from behind her, leaving the rest to trail off. Tori had almost forgotten the other woman was there.

"Just a quick check and I'll be out of your hair," she continued in the same low tone. "Any changes?"

Tori stood staring. "Are you okay?" the virologist said with concern.

"Uh, yeah. Fine." Tori finally replied, fighting her way through her thoughts. "There *is* something, with my eyes," she said, dropping deliberately into a chair as she told Mina what happened.

"Wow. That's not too surprising, though. I mean, their appearance does hint at reflective properties. Do you mind if I darken the room so I can see?"

"Go ahead."

Mina nodded, still tapping her tablet. "So... You were in the arboretum alone with him?" the woman asked, brown eyes flicking up from her tablet then back down.

Tori raised a brow. "Yes."

"Oh." She pushed her glasses up her nose with one finger, lips pursing.

"All night, or—" They both let out a startled yell when the floor suddenly jolted beneath their feet. Mina barely kept herself from falling by gripping one of the chair backs while Tori's hands locked onto the arms, eyes wide.

"*Que demonios*, what was that?" Mina breathed.

The two of them cried out when it happened again, and Tori's first thought was that something had hit the ship. The rooms dimmed, panels above the doors lighting to show the exits.

"Emergency protocol," Tori said, trying to keep calm. Her comm went off almost immediately and she answered just as a third jolt hit them. Mina gasped, bracing herself between the floor and furniture, which was now locked in place.

"Doctor Davis, this is Captain Arya."

"How bad are we hit? Is anyone injured?"

"There's no impact. It's coming from the alien vessel. We have no idea why or wh—" The man's voice cut out then back. "—ur quarantine. You have full clearance to get to that gate and find out what the hell they're doing to my ship!" he barked as another tremor shook them.

The connection ended, and Tori pushed herself up and against the wall, making for the door. "Where are you going? What's happening?" Mina said from the floor.

"Their ship is causing it. I have to get to the gate." As if on cue the doors parted to admit four soldiers. They surrounded her.

"Doctor Davis, we're here to escort you to the gate. Direct orders from Ambassador Wells," one of them said.

The two-minute walk to the bay doors never took so long, and Tori almost fell multiple times. The men and woman accompanying her helped where they could to keep her steady, but jolts to the ship threw them all about the corridor like loose marbles, and the sound of shifting metal had her terrified. Tori wanted to shout with relief when they reached the airlock. She pushed ahead, slapping her hands against the smooth dark metal of the Askari vessel, then waited with bated breath for Henry to do his light trick. They didn't wait long.

The soldiers stayed back, their expressions alternating between awe and angst as another tremor shook the *Amendment*. Where was Aderus? Didn't they realize what was happening?! Unless maybe something was seriously wrong aboard the alien vessel. Her heart plummeted, and blood pounded in her ears just as the dark metal parted and she fell forward.

A hard body and firm grip prevented her from hitting the floor. Tori's gaze caught on several Askari as she righted herself and glanced up, into Aderus's flaming gold eyes.

As if by command, the jarring shakes and shudders ceased.

Chapter Twelve

"While we're all pleased your vessel is restored, those surges damaged multiple systems on this ship. There are five minor hull breaches, countless injuries. Part of this alliance is that you share your knowledge and technology, and we could not have greater need of it than right now. Dealing with damage we sustained helping to repair *your* vessel, I must stress again."

Wells and his entourage were the first to arrive at the gate. Mina and the captain soon after, and Tori noticed more soldiers and guards lined the corridor beyond the airlock. It was probably the least composed she'd seen the diplomat. But being violently tossed about and nearly sucked out into space could do that to a person.

Xaphan, Vepar, Jadar and Krim made up most of the ones she'd seen behind Aderus, who stood near her now. His presence working to calm her as Wells laid it on thick. He was trying to use the incident to force their hand. She knew right away it was a mistake.

Movement to the far back of the gate's connecting chamber drew her attention and Tori blinked. It was the hulking deformed one. He silently bared both rows of teeth when he saw she spotted him, black dappled eyes chilling her bones.

Someone clicked low, forcing her gaze back. The situation was growing more strained by the second. Tori stepped forward, trying to intercede.

"With all due respect, Ambassador, they just told you they'd need another transport," she said. "From what I know of how their technology works, it makes sense. This is no worse than what we'd expect to sustain from a major debris storm. It won't be easy, but its fixable," she finished, glancing briefly at Aderus.

Wells looked far from happy but Tori didn't really care. There had been enough excitement for one day. "Am I right, Captain?" she added, seeking confirmation.

The captain stood stoically; arms crossed. "I'll have to comm the *Phoenix* for a few more hands, but yeah. We can handle it." His response was measured. "For now."

Aderus's fervid gaze moved between her and the ambassador, and she couldn't tell if the intensity she felt coming off him, off all of them, was because of Wells' goading or if it was more related to what she'd sensed when she'd fallen through the airlock. Either way, it was different.

Xaphan said something clipped and Vepar turned to stare at him. The others looked too.

"Show me where your ship bleeds," the orange-eyed Askari finally growled.

The captain shifted, appearing either surprised or uneasy, but Tori instantly perked. "And the food printers?" she blurted, jumping on the opportunity.

"There is plenty of prey in the Earthscape," Aderus said, and her eyes widened, searching his gaze. They'd rather catch and kill their own food than work together on fixing the printers?

"I'd say, for those that help with repairs or agree to spend at least half their time aboard the *Amendment,* that can certainly be arranged," Wells said slowly, the diplomat's careful expression lightening. Captain Arya looked like he was having a harder time following along.

"Representative Vepar, thank you." The words were deliberate, but sincere. "We're extremely grateful for your very generous offer of aid."

***

Tori swiped again through the new wing's schematics; her attention glued to the tablet in her lap as she reached blindly for a steaming mug. There were seventy-five suites that connected directly to the arboretum. Each of those had a second grouping of rooms, like hers. It was more than enough to accommodate all the large, reclusive aliens, if and when they came aboard...

She was in the sitting area of her suite, still technically under confinement. Though, no one seemed to be paying much attention to her anymore. They were all far more concerned with the handful of Askari that would soon be roaming the *Amendment* at will—and to think, she'd seen Wells persuading Aderus aboard for less than twenty-four hours as their big breakthrough.

Captain Arya made the announcement shortly after the gathering at the gate, once the energy pulses from the Askari vessel had completely subsided. It was as if the transport's arrival started a chain reaction, she reflected, and now they were all scrambling to keep up. Vepar was looking at the breaches, others wanted into the arboretum. And here she was, stuck in her quarters. It had taken Tori all her reserve not to argue the orders but Dr. Yin didn't want her having free rein of the ship until her condition was more certain. They outweighed a human by Goddess knew how much and could decapitate one with a single blow. So, the idea of her not being there to defend and diffuse things really worried her.

Much of the *Amendment* was on edge, anxious about coming face to face with one of them in the corridors. Worried about how they should act, what they should say. But Tori had been working closely with their extraterrestrial allies for the better part of a month now. Hopefully exposing them to enough human mannerisms and behavior that she had to believe things would go well.

These first would be the easiest, at least; they were the ones she saw most often. There was also the huge advantage that many would likely only come aboard at night, since it was the arboretum that interested them. Combined with the Askari's natural predilection for stealth and seclusion, Tori doubted most humans would even know they were there, and not everyone one had access to the new wing anyway.

She scribbled down a quick note to recheck those restrictions as she sipped, savoring the tea's spicy taste. She was working on a list of things she knew would be a problem or that would discourage them from using the rooms, because the ultimate goal was still the same: integration.

The food printers were a top—if not *the* top—concern, but Tori relegated them to the side for now. Without Askari involvement, there was little progress to be made, and they all seemed far more interested in hunting the arboretum than trying to manipulate human technology to produce something semi-palatable. Which gave her pause.

Tori knew the same alloy from the transports were being used to build new destroyers, but surely anything man-made wasn't going to hold up very long against more advanced alien engineering? Which meant at some point, they would *have* to incorporate Askari technology.

It made her start to appreciate the tactics Wells was taking, though the approach was risky. The faster they could integrate and acclimate the Askari, the more it would reassure Earth governments and the more quickly things could develop.

A small noise interrupted her thoughts and Tori's gaze shot to the open door to the adjoining suite.

She set her tablet down, nerves fluttering. There was *a lot* going on and dealing with it had helped to distract her. But it was almost impossible not to think about the fact Aderus was probably still on the ship. If not now then at some point. She was trying really hard not to dwell on it or about what the outcomes of today might actually mean—they'd have to give their new guests time to adjust, see how things played out. The other half of the equation was purely personal.

When she'd given in to him yesterday in the woods, agreed to accept things for what they were, it was like she'd given herself permission to embrace her feelings, and a part of her was terrified at what that revealed...

Tori reached for her drink then. Gulping the rest down against the sudden tightness in her throat. This was exactly what she vowed she *wouldn't* do. She absolutely refused to torture herself. Instead she listened closely, but heard no other sounds.

Something must have fallen or shifted from all the chaos earlier, she figured, which is when an idea hit her. She pushed to her feet and peeked into the other suite, deliberating for all of five seconds. An hour or two later, Tori had most of the space cleared. She packed whatever she could neatly into designated storage areas, and anything too big or that she couldn't find a place for, she moved to her own suite.

Only two chairs and a stool at the kitchen counter remained when she finished, but it was amazing how much bigger the space felt. She padded back to her own sitting area. Adding a final note to the list of things she felt would make them more comfortable. *Clear rooms.*

Dinner was spent trying to think of foods that tasted like *rukhhal* and dialing them up on the food printer. She knew Mina and Yin were still busy treating injuries from this morning and it made Tori batty she wasn't there helping. She consoled herself by sending the ambassador her report but rubbed her forehead when his response was asking if she'd made progress with the covering. She was still somewhat torn by the idea.

Tori set the tablet down, deciding she needed a break and the smell of air that wasn't artificial. She hesitated only a moment before stepping out into the arboretum. The light had just begun to fade, and she scanned the area, looking for any Askari.

Tori stood like that for some time; arms crossed, watching the forest. She stayed close to the access, and when an animal cried in the distance, she started, willing to bet it was one of them. A blue-green glow lit her arms as Henry responded and she looked down, slowly unfolding her arms.

Could she control it?

Deciding it wouldn't hurt to try she steadied her footing and held out her arms...imagining the waves of light in her mind and willing them to appear.

Nothing happened.

Tori's shoulders sagged, and she frowned. Inhaling deeply, she tried again. Closing her eyes.

An abrupt punch of vibration shook her body as she jumped, loosing a sharp cry. Then her lips parted at the bright energy that flowed down the *havat*, just like she had envisioned. Her eyes widened with excitement before the crunching of gravel made her jerk up. Tori tensed, until she saw who it was.

"Hey. Did you just—" The words were torn from her as Aderus literally swept her backward into the suite. The smoky bite of his scent teasing her nose. Her feet flailed, and she grasped quickly at him for balance but he held her effortlessly, clawed hands engulfing her ribs. "Aderus!!" she exclaimed into his torso.

"*They watch*," he hissed over her ear.

"Who does?"

"The others, and your people."

So, they did have it monitored. *Hopefully that's not the case farther in*. She thought, a blush scorching her cheeks. Tori quickly focused on the first part of his response.

"The others already know. They've been on the receiving end, remember?" She said, blowing a strand of hair from her face.

He moved back, sharp features an unreadable mask. "You are trying to control it. Why?"

"You have to ask me that? Because it's dangerous," she said earnestly. "I really hurt you. But if you want the answer you're looking for." She hesitated. "Then yes, Wells feels we need it. In case things get out of hand."

She whispered the last part, searching his ethereal eyes for any bit of trust or affection. When he retreated another step with a short series of clicks, Tori snapped. Her lips thinned, and she clenched her jaw. "I see. Well, there's certainly an easy solution to this problem. I'll be right back," she said, and turned to march back into her rooms. She made for the bedroom, snatched a pair of panties then strode back out. His gleaming gold eyes were scanning the room when she returned. Likely just having noticed the change in scenery. He drew up as she approached, tresses expanding.

Tori stopped in front of him, bending to quickly slide the panties up her legs. Henry pulsed weakly when she straightened, feeling for the disc at the base of her neck. She banded her breasts with one arm as the material slid up her body, having been too flustered to deal with a bra, then mimicked the movements of his long fingers when he'd shown her how to remove it. This time it worked. The disc peeled reluctantly from her skin and Tori swallowed, handing it gently to Aderus.

"Here."

Chapter Thirteen

Aderus struggled mightily not to be distracted as his eyes roamed greedily over Tori's face and body. When she'd stalked up to him, he'd been expecting her to attack and his instincts automatically responded. Too aroused by the idea to notice that was not her intention.

Instead she shocked him by removing her *havat*. He stared down at it, resting starkly within her palm.

"I told you before. I would never intentionally hurt any of you, and if that's what you think of me then take it back," she said in wavering mono-tone. "I'm serious. I don't want it."

He searched her pale, flat features again but could only sense her resolve, and it made something shift inside him. The *khurzha* just handed him Earth's greatest advantage, willingly exposing herself to weakness. She understood its power, knew her people coveted it; all to make a point. He could trust her.

Aderus loosed a low throaty rumble, noting her exotic eyes glistened with more than inner light as he clasped the disc between his claws and lifted his hand. She jerked back, pinning him with a hard look. It made his *vryll* ruffle. Then he placed the disc back onto her skin, watching her rounded nostrils flare.

She looked between his eyes, perhaps trying to determine his intent as her chest began to rise and fall and a surge of her scent tickled his snout. The smack of something tight around his wrist a moment later stunned him. Aderus's gaze shot down, seeing her small pale fingers wrapped around his flesh.

His body responded, *pvost* coiling painfully behind his *vryll* as it ignited the space between them. He pushed forward with a snarl, narrowly reminding himself to show restraint. "No," she said, when he attempted to turn her and a flash of darkened skin caught his gaze. Then the hand banding her hills of flesh let go to fondle him boldly between the legs.

Aderus snapped his teeth, pulling his wrist from her grip; she always seemed to want to touch him there. He burrowed his claws into her fine tresses with a series of warning clicks, fingers wrapping firmly around the arm that held him before she offhanded him again—stepping close to press her body up and into his. Her head tipped back, glowing eyes entrancing him. Then he felt her delicate fingers at the side of his neck and knew what she was after. He gave it to her, willing the material up his body.

The corners of her lips curled while the hand on his lower half pressed into him. The *khurzha* looked down. "I can feel you moving," she uttered and he clicked his teeth again. Walking them into the half wall they called a *counter*, right before his *havat* exposed him to her touch. Tori stumbled, stretched as she was against him, and grasped the tresses at the back of his neck sharply to keep from falling. Between it and the firm strokes to his sensitive bulge, Aderus froze, the claws of one foot scraping the floor just as he felt her short fingers slip over his *vryll*. He'd intended to knock her hand away, the feeling still too foreign and intense, but his body wasn't responding to those commands. It craved whatever she wanted to inflict upon him with relish, his slick folds already open and on full display. He hissed long and low, grip spasming on her arm and tresses.

"*Goddess,*" she breathed, staring between them. "I never thought this would be such a fucking turn on, but you're beautiful, Aderus."

Her soft fingers slicked up and down and his *pvost* whipped viciously within his body. His skin felt cold as he struggled to keep it contained. He didn't know why he wanted to prolong the pleasure-pain of her touches but then he snorted as her needing scent nearly suffocated him and his *pvost* broke free. Actually wrapping around her hand in its eagerness. Tori jerked and made a startled sound, her fingers seizing at his nape. Aderus was too focused on finding her opening, however, as thoughts of it and breeding her filled his mind. His jaw chafed the top of her head.

"Let go," she panted as the seeking part of him brushed the thin covering at her hips. He blinked and snarled when he felt her release him. She braced her arms behind her then bucked her hips up and onto the platform. His *pvost* grazing the bare flesh of her thighs in its efforts to reach her.

Aderus clicked and pressed forward. Her legs were now splayed; the skin of her chest and cheeks a faint red. She reached for him again, holding his gaze as her other hand slipped beneath the scrap that hid her center. "Come here," she said. The spines up his arms, legs and back stiffening as his *pvost* surged between her fingers. He watched the covering lift and move, and a strong swell of her scent followed. She was petting herself as she had the first time, he realized. The tapered tip of him used the opportunity to slip beneath the senseless constraint, and her soft cavern clenched as he squeezed inside.

"Wait," she gasped, eyes fluttering. Aderus hissed and jerked when her fingers delved deeply into his folds. The intense sensation making his *pvost* retract as her hand dropped to cover her opening. He brayed fiercely, eyes blazing down at her.

"That's better, eyes on mine." Her voice was rough, and Aderus flashed his teeth when her leg latched onto his hip. The breath billowed from his chest. He searched her expressive face, trying to understand her actions.

"I want to see you, and I want you to see me."

Her fingers stroked him then and his *pvost* responded. The tapered tip feeling mindfully around her hand, which still barred her opening. Tori's eyes suddenly shot wide and she yelled, a second leg wrapping around his hips.

"Do that again," she demanded, fingers curling inside him. Aderus hissed at the sensation, eyes closing briefly.

His tip slicked over and around her modest folds, their fine outer bristles tickling his sensitive flesh. The appendage had none of the protections of his outer skin.

"There!" she breathed, legs spasming. He felt a slight bump. "Small circles around it." Her fingers in his folds mimed the motion, and for some reason it incited him. She may not be able to give him the satisfaction of a fight, but this was a different kind of dance, Aderus ceded. Claws smoothing along the skin of her inner arm. True to airs, Tori commanded him with words and bold touches, and he seemed to revel in it more each time they bred.

Blue orbs locked with his and she began to tremble. Aderus's tresses rose and his irises narrowed, reluctant to concede the strange contest. Then he tensed as a *krhune* erupted from his throat.

"*Aderus.*"

Tori was shaking now. Her fingers spasming inside his body as his tip slid over and around the bump of flesh. Her striking eyes widened, swimming with some kind of liquid, and an odd feeling gripped him. It was as if she were reaching inside him, with more than just her fingers.

The light cut out as they slammed closed with a loud sound and Tori curled into him. Legs wrapping tightly about his hips, while the hand in his folds tore away to grab fiercely at his back. It released him from whatever hold he'd been under and Aderus hissed. His claws scraped against the top of the half wall as his *pvost* pushed through her idle fingers, tearing the stupid scrap of clothing. She cried out again when he breached her, clicking his teeth at the tight cinching feel. Her hips bucked in time with the clenches, and Aderus leaned forward, fighting his way through to get deeper inside.

"*Oh Gods*," Tori rasped into his torso. The sounds from his throat grew, shaking his chest. He tried to subdue them, but the feel of her gripping him overpowered anything else, and when her other hand turned to lazily cup his folds Aderus's muscles began to twitch and shudder.

"Come for me, baby," she said right before her fingers delved deep and Aderus let go of her tresses to crush the ledge of the platform with a snorted snarl. He nudged her roughly as his body released, seed flowing into and from her small cavern. His long tongue swiped her neck, craving the taste.

Tori jolted. "Gentle," she said when he burrowed into her shoulder.

He didn't heed much until the flood gripping him eased and his *pvost* writhed sluggishly. Aderus opened his eyes. She'd wrapped herself around him, chest jostling his for breath. As if the *khurzha* sensed his sudden unease, her arms dropped, and a glimpse of contrasting color caught his attention again.

Aderus straightened, hissing softly. Tori noticed the direction of his gaze and reached up to cover the area...it was where she'd fed him, he realized.

"It's fine. Just a little bruised."

Aderus blinked. He'd not fully appreciated how much more delicate she was until that moment. Something his own body would have healed without thought, marred and discolored her skin for *sols* after.

"It actually looks much better than it should," she murmured.

He thought of when she fed him and those feelings ran through him. Feeding could be intimate. The greater the risk, the more meaningful the act. Tori knew how much it would take to heal; she'd known in the Earthscape. The awareness triggered a powerful urge and Aderus looked down at where they were still joined, nostrils flaring. Her legs gripped him loosely, sending a current of heat through his center. And when one of them slipped down his backside, Aderus acted.

Tori made a sound of alarm as he gasped her hips, dragging them from the half wall and onto the floor with a clipped growl. She didn't fight him when he flipped her to face it and his length pulled out of her. Instead her legs folded completely, and she dropped back onto her heels, elbows holding her weight. Aderus's eyes flamed. She spoke, acting startled but lax, and he realized she had no idea what she'd just done. Her chest was practically touching the floor and the deference it signaled, were she Askari, had no equal. He'd never experienced the like with a female.

Aderus surged over her with a rolling bray, his longer legs sliding astride hers, mimicking the posture. His *vryll* was still parted, folds laving the soft flesh of her backside. Tori jerked when his *pvost* found her again.

A thought worked its way through his clouded brain. Aderus withdrew, the tip of him feeling further along for the small bump. She jolted hard when he did, and the top of her head slammed into his jaw from below. Aderus hissed, pushing her arms out. His plated chest covered her back and he reveled in the feel of her stretched beneath him.

She was speaking again. "...hear me? I don't think I can," she drowsed.

The words lacked conviction, however, as he felt her hips writhe. He clicked low, nudging her flesh insistently. Tori began to pant and moan. His tresses spilled over them, and Aderus could see her wound. The more he stared at it, the more the feelings gripping him grew.

"Too much. I can't," she said, sounding defeated. He quickly thought of the other touches she had shown him and her responses to them. Then reached beneath her, dragging his roughened fingers over the peaks of her hills. Tori cried out. Her body began to spasm and she dropped her head forward to the floor.

Seeing her willingly perform the gesture reduced him to a single impulse and Aderus barely perceived the vibrations quaking his throat and chest. His *pvost* slicked back, finding her weeping, snug entrance and surged inside. He was vaguely aware of Tori twisting and bucking beneath him as he wedged himself further, unable to focus on anything else.

The muscles of his arms and torso coiled tight after only a few eager pushes. Aderus pressed over her, hissing brokenly with release as sensations both familiar and unsung wracked his body. It made him feel weak, empty.

And in its wake: the stirrings of something entirely new.

Chapter Fourteen

Tori awoke on the floor. Again.

She felt groggy and a little worn, but also so well rested she couldn't remember the last time she'd slept as well. She blinked lazily at a wall in front of her before raising her head in confusion, trying to get oriented. She was lying in the inlet of the adjoining suite's kitchenette. Hidden between the wall and counter. They'd been together once *on* the counter and once on the open floor, but inside the kitchen? Not that she could recall.

She sat up, noting next that Henry covered her body. Aderus must have done it, she thought, fingering her hair. Which meant he must have also moved her. How weird.

Tori spoke aloud to the ship's AI—it was morning. Which almost prompted a mini panic attack until she remembered she was off duty, still confined more or less to her quarters. She pushed to her feet, immediately dialing up some coffee on the food printer then looked around. Not at all surprised her lover was nowhere to be seen. It didn't stop her from giving in to the urge to check the suite's bedroom, however, before shuffling back out to the sitting area with its two lonely chairs.

Sleep-laced visions of him staring down at her flashed through her mind, and she halted. He'd definitely been there. Not sleeping, but, with her for a time. Daylight ruled out the arboretum, so he was probably back aboard their vessel.

Tori plopped onto a stool. A fleeting giddiness gripping her. It felt like something big had happened between them last night. When he'd placed the *havat* back onto her skin, she'd been so overwhelmed by the gesture she attacked him; determined to play out with her body what she couldn't yet say with words. And she wanted to believe he'd felt something too. Because the second time had left her reeling. His urgency, the way he covered her. It seemed deliberate. Not to mention the initiative he'd shown.

It went a long way to assuaging her greatest fear, Tori considered. And that was the thought Aderus may not be able to love her.

Yup. She'd said it.

She wanted to believe he was capable of it. That two intelligent species worlds apart couldn't truly be *that* different. Askari spoke through their actions, and his actions told her he definitely felt *something* for her; she wouldn't have entertained anything with him otherwise. She was just afraid of getting her heart broken. And not through any intentional misdoing on his part, but because he legitimately didn't know how.

Last night had given her hope though. And she forced the worry aside. It wasn't as if she didn't have her own intimacy issues. One too many failed relationships and a job that demanded most of her time had left her a little emotionally reticent, which forced a laugh. ...They might be more alike than she realized.

Twenty minutes later she'd returned to her rooms, showered, and was just looking at her messages when Mina commed.

"I wanted to check nothing's changed. Comm if you need anything, but we're still a little overwhelmed here," the virologist said quickly, her slight accent more pronounced.

Tori pressed her lips together, feeling useless. "You know I would be there if I could."

"Of course. Jadar actually offered to help." Tori's brows rose at that. "You just focus on you. I think we could be close to some real answers. That is if that—" Mina broke into fluent Spanish and Tori couldn't make out the words. They sounded irritated, though, so she didn't push. The call was short, for obvious reasons, and once Mina disconnected Tori went back to checking her messages. She walked into the connecting suite, attention on her tablet as a sound briefly distracted her.

Apparently, a few trees had fallen in the arboretum and the captain was advising against passengers using it until the debris could be cleared. Tori looked up when she heard the noise again and frowned. It was coming from the access and sounded like a muffled voice.

She hesitated only an instant before issuing a command to open it. Someone was standing on the other side: he was young, around her height.

"What are you doing?"

He started when she spoke, looking up from his own tablet. "Oh, I didn't know anyone had been assigned to these rooms."

"Mine are the ones connecting these, but these rooms are being used. I'm Dr. Davis. What are you doing?" she said again, nodding to his tablet. Tori stayed where she was, speaking to him through the open doorway.

"I'm just checking the feeds. Captain's orders," he said.

"These rooms aren't supposed to be monitored. An Askari is using them."

That seemed to fluster him. "Uh, yes. That's what I have. But it says only the interior feeds, these are exterior."

Semantics. That was definitely Wells.

Tori's gaze caught movement on the man's tablet just then, and her eyes widened. The image had been fleeting but there was no doubt. It was the pale-skinned male with crimson eyes. "I've treated him," she said, pointing. "Is that feed from the arboretum?"

He grew guarded and a bit flustered again. "Uh, yeah. That one was here before any of the rest of them," he said, looking down.

"The access feeds are synced to the ones along the path, so we can kind of track their movements," he said distractedly, still watching the vid. "But, man, I've never seen an animal move like that."

"They're not animals. They're people." She responded, watching him carefully.

"I know that." He blinked. "I'm just saying..."

The conversation stuck with Tori the rest of the day, as did what she'd learned. So the male she helped had been aboard the *Amendment* for some time. Why would they hide something like that?? Did Aderus know?

She entered the arboretum again as evening approached and the simulated light of day faded. A hunch told her it was doubtful the captain's advisory would pertain to the Askari. A few downed trees was nothing to them, and from what she'd heard, interest in the "Earthscape" had only grown. Most passengers didn't wander the conserve past dark anyway, so there was little chance of that being an issue.

She strode down the path, wondering where he was as she sensed at least one pair of eyes.

It had been discovered that they could communicate through their *havats*. Tori still didn't quite understand how, but it made her wish she had pushed the issue with Aderus, and she would. She'd just been too busy handling other things. He always seemed to find her though. Maybe Henry was communicating and she didn't even realize it.

Speaking of which, Tori stopped. The light he emitted had grown, like someone had suddenly turned up the intensity. And as darkness fell it lit the whole space around her a good few feet in diameter. She was so focused on it and the way it began to blind her that she heard Aderus before she saw him.

"Others are preying." The rough rumble made her tense, but not from unease. "Control your aura."

Tori looked up, unsure of whether he'd slunk from the brush or dropped down from the branches. His pupils were pinpoints and both rows of teeth flashed when he spoke.

"I was just going to ask you what's going on with it. I don't exactly like being blinded either."

Aderus stepped close with a rolling click. "Quiet this," he gruffed, raising long-clawed fingers to lightly touch her temple, "and the *havat* will follow." His arm lowered slowly, and Tori swallowed.

She didn't know if what happened last night was making her imagine things, but a softness, dare she say tenderness, rippled through her. She closed her eyes and tried to do as he said. Tori sensed the light dim from behind her eyelids and when she opened them again Henry was back to his usual glow.

"I don't get it. That never happened before," she murmured.

Aderus's gaze darted up and behind her, one ear flicking. Tori turned her head. The idea that one of them might be watching from the trees made her skin pimple.

"Our ship is healed, its energies amplified." She turned back at the deep sound of his voice. "You think too loudly now."

Tori blinked. What he said implied the material was connected to their ship. Looking back, the notion didn't surprise her. That wave of light down the corridor walls right after Henry's first energy pulse was just too coincidental. And she knew their technology reacted to thought and emotion, but now he was telling her that ability was amplified? It was a little overwhelming and seemed like a lot to manage.

"I need to talk to you," she whispered. Still digesting what he said. "Do you know of somewhere there aren't feeds?"

Tori watched his eyes move over her. When he *snikted* and turned to walk into the brush, she followed. They walked quietly for a time, the only noise from their feet as they moved beneath the canopy. Well, *her* feet. Aderus was easily more than twice her size but he practically glided over the ground, each step eliciting little to no sound. Tori watched him, endeavoring not to fall flat on her face. If she tried to do that, they'd be here all night, but the fluid way his body moved had her struggling to keep pace most of the way.

Tori came up behind him when he suddenly halted. She'd been looking down and made a startled sound, hands lightly grazing his back to catch herself. He hissed softly. The muscles beneath his *havat* unyielding as his ears stood erect through his tresses.

"No one watches here," he said.

Tori looked around wide-eyed. "How do you know?"

"I know," he rumbled, turning slowly.

"Did you know the light-skinned male has been in the arboretum since right after my eyes changed and I was quarantined?

Aderus's eyes sparked, thick braids rustling. He bit out a word, but it didn't seem directed at her. "Why speak of him?"

Tori's brows drew together as she stared up at him. "Because no one said anything, I just found out today. Why would they have hidden it? And on a related note, why do you all seem to treat him so differently? Jadar didn't even know his name and didn't seem to care. I know you two *disputed*, but Braxas is just as violent, and I can tell he dislikes me more."

He looked away with a rolling click when her little oration ended, as if he'd momentarily lost interest. He didn't want to talk about this for some reason. "Aderus?"

Glowing gold eyes locked with hers, then moved between them. "He is *palkriv*," he growled.

"Okay, and what does that mean?"

"His traits are undesirable, so he is ignored and lives between worlds."

Undesirable? The only thing different about him was the color of his skin and it triggered a memory. Aderus had pointed out her pallor while trying (and failing miserably) to "woo" her. Along with every other "unattractive" feature. The way the male seemed fixated on her skin, the apparent connection she'd felt; it was like he was searching for acceptance. And since his *own* species shunned him... Her knee-jerk reaction was disgust and Tori's jaw clenched, but she crossed her arms over her chest, wanting to understand it.

"Why undesirable, exactly?" She sensed the glow from Henry brighten.

Aderus drew up. "Why do you speak of him?" he said again. It smacked of jealousy. Were he human she'd be sure of it.

"I'm trying to understand," she responded. "Humans have different colors too, you know. We've learned the hard way it's wrong to treat someone unequally just because of the way they look. I'm attracted to you *because* of your differentness, Aderus, not in spite of it. So, tell me why it matters?"

His eyes flicked over her body again, looking for something but she couldn't say what. He must have found it, though, because he answered.

"We will always yearn to hunt. It is our nature, and a measure of strength and ability. All of Askara's terrain is dark, the atmosphere thinner. Those born with your color cannot blend and their skin is weak. It blisters, becomes diseased. The purpose of breeding is to produce strong progeny."

Of course. Everything came back to weakness with them. It seemed like such a contradiction; how a comparably advanced race could still be so primitive when it came to matters of emotion and culture.

"I see." She nodded, trying to keep her feelings in check. The explanation helped but that didn't excuse anything. "Well, those things have no relevance here and there aren't any females, so I fail to see why he should be treated any different."

"There *are* females." Aderus responded, pushing close.

The rough purr distracted her, despite Tori's best efforts. And when his meaning registered her heart skipped. Compared to how he'd first viewed her, what he said was more than a compliment and it sparked some pretty heavy emotions. Tori looked down, fighting through them.

A twig snapped, and heat from his body suddenly blanketed her as a soft growl stirred the hair at the crown of her head. It sent tingles along her skin and she inhaled, breathing his unique smell. When her hands began to twitch with the sudden need to touch him, she didn't fight it. Instead she swallowed, lifting them to settle gently against his stomach as the flesh beneath her fingers jumped.

The air shifted, and then Tori froze when claws caught and held abruptly along her backside, followed by the heavy weight of his hands. She felt a hesitant bump to her forehead, Aderus's fingers flex into her hips...and literally couldn't breathe. Not wanting to risk disturbing what was possibly their first real intimate moment.

Her eyes closed, nose practically touching his chest.

Tori hadn't realized how much she wanted this. How voraciously she'd hungered for it, until her lip began to tremble, and she swallowed painfully this time, pushing her face into his torso.

To her shock and pleasure, Aderus didn't pull away. Instead he rumbled low, bumping her forehead lightly again until Tori released her breath: slowly, to center herself. If she blubbered all over him now, she doubted he'd be eager to repeat the experience.

The glow from Henry had brightened with the force of her emotions, and Tori ignored it as a light touch grazed the back of her neck. She assumed it was Aderus, rooting around, but the second touch came as more of a knocking, causing her to frown. Her eyes flew open as soon as she realized what it was.

Bugs!! Henry was attracting bugs!

Tori squealed. Pushing into and around Aderus's large body as he snarled, likely confused and startled. Then he hissed deeply when she shimmied, trying her best to avoid the moth that seemed determined to dive bomb her face.

Yeah, it was stupid. And a total mood killer, she lamented. But Tori couldn't help herself, the thing was huge!

"Get it away!" she exclaimed, toes curling inside her *havat*.

Aderus clicked and brayed. She felt his body propel her backward and something hard butt her hip before a large hand came down on her chest. At the same time she watched his free hand snatch quickly at the air. There was virtually no hesitation—Aderus put it in his mouth.

"Oh, gross," she said, face twisting as she ceased all struggles. "I can't believe—are you sure that was even edible?" Her brows rose in concern.

Instead of answering he continued to watch the air, crunching on the first unfortunate victim. When another flew close by, he snatched that one too.

Tori watched on dumbly. The large Askari seemed completely enthralled, and she swore she heard that throat-clearing hum at least once as he held her still, taking total advantage of her mental impotence. *Is he amused, or just pleased by the damn menu?* She thought, reaching to cover her eyes. It was as much to block the view as to keep from laughing, but in all seriousness, this wasn't funny! It was traumatic and disgusting!! You know, for the bugs.

Eventually, Tori got Henry under control. There were few incentives more powerful than wanting to avoid being covered in insects. Her taste for the outdoors, however, was more than satisfied and she asked Aderus to show her back to the path.

She trailed behind him, moving much slower this time. Her mind ran, but Tori chose to ignore it; she still had to focus on her steps. Her night vision might be amazingly improved, but Aderus seemed to move no differently than in the daylight. He stopped twice along the way, acting as if he'd seen or heard something, but would watch as she caught up to him. It both amused and excited her.

When they stepped onto the path, she fidgeted. "The doors to my rooms are open, if you want to stop by when you're done. Even if it's just to sleep."

Aderus blinked down at her. His luminous gaze didn't waver as he lifted his chin, clicking softly. Tori guessed what he might be looking for, but this wasn't about that.

Be honest. You wouldn't say no.

Tori swallowed. No, she wouldn't. The sex between them was unlike anything she'd ever imagined, in a really good way. But his kind didn't have romantic relationships, which meant they probably didn't sleep together. Or so she'd assumed.

In fact, she knew very little about his sleeping habits.

"That room by the access is a bedroom, you know. I looked for you there when I woke this morning. Where have you been sleeping?"

He didn't answer her but to stare, and Tori felt a stab of disappointment. His eyes, however, were just as intense as always and it reminded her of when they first met. Right before he'd asked her to come aboard their ship.

"Well, *I'd* like it if it were just to sleep. Call it a human thing," she said with a weak smile and walked around him toward the access.

Did she want him to stop her? Grab her by the arm with a hissed growl and carry her into the suite for crazy alien sex, followed by some actual intimacy? Of course, she did! But not as a result of forcing him to be something he wasn't. And Tori didn't expect any less for herself.

"Oh!" she said, stopping abruptly. "Did you move me this—" But then cut off as she turned back and saw that no one was there.

Of course, she thought with a sigh.

Chapter Fifteen

Tori awoke later that night, oddly alert. It was the second time. She'd intentionally left the door to her bedroom open, as well as the adjoining access; trying not to expect anything, but it was likely why she wasn't sleeping well. She reached up to remove her sleep mask. Grateful for the thing now that her eyes picked up on every little bit of light, then swung her legs off the side of the bed as she paused, listening.

Wishful thinking. He's not here, an inner voice taunted. Tori wondered if perhaps he had been, though, and that's what had woken her.

She waddled into the bathroom to relieve herself, feeling gingerly for the faucet. The thought that something hot might help her to relax impelled her past the bed and out into the common area.

"Tablet, on," she mumbled as the device powered up somewhere close by, and she used the light to guide her. The floor felt cold on her bare feet and she stumbled, too occupied with debating whether she wanted to activate Henry or not.

"You made less noise in the Earthscape," a voice rumbled, and Tori gasped, looking for the source. Aderus stood along the far wall near the access. Her shoulders lowered.

"You could have told me you were out here," she croaked, heart skipping with excitement now instead of fright. He seemed to blend seamlessly with the shadows, she noted, except for the glittering gold of his eyes.

He didn't answer but to raise his chin, a soft sound sparking her ardor. Tori chose to ignore it, focusing instead on something safe as she rested a hand on one chairback.

"Trouble sleeping?" she asked, voice still rough from slumber. Her fingers curled when he left the wall to move opposite her across the small table.

He would either shoot her down again or choose to talk, she thought. Tori really hoped for the latter. Especially when he regarded her with what felt like an entirely new spirit of connection.

"We do not nest as humans do," he growled softly.

"I kind of figured that. You're never there when I wake… " Her legs bent to rest carefully on the chair arm, thinking sluggish as she chose her words. "If by nest, you mean sleep together, then yes, couples will do that. But mostly it's the comfort of knowing someone's nearby. Sleeping, resting, eating." Tori paused. "It's why I kept the doors open. Though I usually sleep alone, too." That last bit might be true, but it felt like it was more for a little self-preservation.

"I was concerned where you'd been sleeping because I care, Aderus," she added thickly, and wanted to say *a lot.* "It wasn't an interrogation."

The faint shimmer from his *havat* gave his shape an almost dream-like appearance. Making her question how he'd blended so thoroughly into the darkness, before the deep tones of his voice forced her attention back.

"Resting space is private. Because it is the only time we are vulnerable. Those words threaten, were you Askari."

She understood the hesitation now, and sat quietly for a moment, considering what he'd said. Then she stood, bridging the gap between them to stop close enough that the heat from his body warmed her. The urge to touch him again nearly had her slapping her own hands away.

"That's not how I meant them. And 'nesting' does have its advantages, you know" she murmured, raising her gaze as he clicked low and shifted. Tori kissed her hand, placing it gently on his chest.

"You wouldn't be vulnerable with me."

***

Mina comm-ed early the next morning. Tori had barely gotten out of bed and changed when the device went off. She knew there were bags beneath her eyes but some things were worth a little sleep deprivation.

After she placed her hand on his chest, Tori had surprised even herself when she'd walked into the kitchen, grabbed a hot drink and returned to bed with a grin and whispered "Goodnight." And Aderus had watched her every step of the way. The intensity from his ethereal stare giving her all the confirmation she needed that she'd made the right choice. Tori had practically *heard* his mind working as she sat in bed, senses straining to determine if he was still there while half expecting him to slink into her room. The notion was oddly comforting. She hadn't shared quarters with someone since Liv and it reminded her how much she missed it. Eventually she'd dozed off, empty cup in hand.

"I'm on my way. And I have answers." Mina's pressing tone made Tori anxious. It didn't take long for the main entry to chime. She invited the other woman into the sitting area, sensing it'd be necessary.

"Who else knows?" Tori said as they sat. That would tell her how serious it was.

"I filed a report, Wells and Yin, but I wouldn't call it bad, so you can relax. Your confinement is officially lifted. That's good, right?" Mina's glasses slipped down her nose as her brows rose with the bright tone.

"Thank Gaia," Tori breathed. Sitting around all day, trying to occupy herself was just not who she was. Especially considering all that had happened since she'd regained consciousness.

A tablet was in the virologist's lap, but she looked at Tori as she spoke. "We analyzed your samples from when you were having the symptoms, Jadar and me."

Tori drew up. "So, you're working together. That's great."

Mina waved her off awkwardly. "I had an idea after reading a report," she said, looking to the little black disc of her *havat* at the base of her neck. "And it's not a virus. It's that covering."

A chill ran down Tori's spine and she reached for it, unable to help herself. Henry was warm to the touch and loosed a small vibration. "How do you know? I mean, I was wearing it before, when they scanned me.

"Their technology, its abilities seem tied to the condition of their ship," Mina explained, her voice lowering. "And since that transport, readings have been off the charts. It's got Wells and above on edge because I don't think they had any idea." The other woman shook her head. "As for the Askari, they didn't know what they were looking for. Jadar said they've never had their tech respond to another species like this, but he suspected it after the first energy pulse."

Tori's gaze grew unfocused, recalling the fear, shock then gratitude she'd felt when Henry saved her aboard their vessel. "That was days ago," she replied.

Mina shifted. "Yeah, there's been a lot going on...and I wouldn't give him access to the samples until he agreed to let me back on their ship." She said the second part quickly and Tori blinked, impressed by the woman's tenacity.

As a scientist, she'd thought of it briefly as a possibility, but a virus had seemed far more likely. Technology that could respond to thought wasn't outside the realm of theory, after all, just practice. So, she never gave much credence to the idea it was the *havat* that had "infected" her. And why should she? That was the behavior of a living organism. She voiced as much to Mina.

"*Exactly!*" The other woman's expression sparked with enthusiasm and her eyes glazed. "Which is something because—" She broke off, seeming to catch herself. "Or, never mind. I think we've only scratched the surface. But you seem stable, and now we know the cause."

"Is it reversible? Did Jadar say? I could undergo gene treatments," Tori said, a part of her rejecting the idea as soon as she said it.

Mina frowned. "I wouldn't. You know as well as I do those therapies can be dangerous, especially with something unknown like this. Unless it becomes life threatening, I wouldn't do anything."

"And my symptoms before? Those weren't cause for concern?" Tori said, getting agitated.

"As best we can tell they were the new genes reacting to changes in your body, normal fluctuations in hormones." Mina shrugged. "We'll keep an eye on it. Have they returned?" she said with genuine concern.

"Not yet," Tori mumbled.

The virologist smiled tightly, then stood. "Would it help if I told you I might envy you a little?"

Tori looked at her with a barked laugh. "Just let me know when you're ready to trade places. It's not as glamorous as it seems."

"I've seen," Mina chuckled. "Still."

"Still," Tori agreed with a small smile.

Mina invited her for a drink in the new rec annex before she left, which warmed Tori; her fingers straying to Henry once more. Considering everything the virologist just told her, she should at least be disturbed by it. But the only sense she got, from the instant Aderus gave it to her, was one of comfort and assurance. Those feelings had grown, she admitted, in spite of some reluctance on her part. It was alien, unknown, unpredictable. Yet her gut told Tori to trust it, even embrace it. Just as she'd decided to embrace a relationship with Aderus; whatever that might mean.

The sudden urge it sparked was how she found herself looking for him at the gate a short time later. A niggling sensation somehow having pointed her in that direction. She waited patiently while Henry pulsed—excitedly, it seemed to her now—and the airlock parted. Aderus stood staring down at her.

"There's something I need to see... Please."

Chapter Sixteen

They were readying for the next transport. One that would finish forming the first hybridized vessels, yet Aderus was unfocused.

His kind's connection with their technology was sacred, but never did it alter their makeup, as he learned it had with her. What Jadar said caused more questions than answers, and the healer seemed completely absorbed in his workings to uncover them. Aderus left him to, tracking back toward the Earth vessel when his *havat* alerted him to Tori's presence at the airlock.

"There's something I need to see... Please. I want you to show me Askara."

The words evoked a dangerously satisfying feeling. He searched the *khurzha's* blended eyes, then measured her body's language. She was not upset or angry; rather, earnest, and he only sensed sincerity.

Tori grasped his fingers without hesitation as they entered decontamination and Aderus looked down curiously. His muscles didn't so much as twitch. Instead her touch felt expected, and the thought teased him as they entered the passageways.

What happened in the Earthscape had kept him from resting, as did her actions and words. They played on his mind, making Aderus consider things he never had before...like when he curled his fingers into her backside, drawing close on an impulse he didn't fully understand. She'd pushed her face into his chest, responding strongly, it seemed. Before reacting crazily to the harmless and savory Earth flies.

The feelings those moments stirred, however, was what found him seeking her out later in her living space—what he'd shared he spoke of only with her; and none before her, he admitted ominously.

"Wow. So, this is what you meant," he heard her say, trying to keep slightly ahead in case they came across any of the others. It reminded him that she'd never seen their vessel unbroken. Frequent waves of light now lit the corridors, the walls pulsing with vitality. Some called it an awareness.

"It's making my skin tingle," she said, and Aderus glanced back. She'd retracted her *havat* beneath loose Earth clothes, the pale flesh of her arms bare. He turned with a low hiss. The others were threatened when she wore it, as was he before, but seeing her so openly vulnerable bothered him more, he realized.

"Why are you not wearing your *havat*?"

Tori looked down, seeming surprised. "I won't wear it again until I know I can control it," she said evenly. "I can't expect you or any of the others to trust me when I don't even trust myself."

"And if we dispute?"

"I trust *you*." She smiled and Aderus blinked.

"Let's hope we're past that," she said, pushing her tresses behind one ear.

He looked forward again, reflecting on her words, and brought Tori to the same space he'd shown her his home for the first time. Only now the view would not be from afar. He spoke aloud in his native tongue, watching the transformation surround them. It wasn't an easy sight. He didn't do this often because of the emotions it stirred. The likeness was of Askara before the *Maekhur* invasion, and Aderus became still, watching along with her.

She was quiet at first, lips parting. Aderus snorted. His home world had that effect, he thought proudly.

"Ohhh, my—it's..."

As he measured her reaction the feeling within him shifted, evolved. He hadn't felt the same since their last breeding. Tori occupied his thoughts, same as before, but nothing about her seemed foreign anymore. In truth, it was just the opposite: each different thing she showed him made more sense, as if belonging to him too, and Aderus didn't know what to call it other than a knowing.

The *khurzha's* gaze locked onto him then, and his spines rippled with the change in her body.

"When the destroyers are ready, I want to go with you."

The words were murmured but the look she gave was that of a battle mien. Aderus hissed softly, feeling his eyes brighten.

***

The sight of Askara rendered Tori speechless. She thought she'd done a decent job imagining, but the "reality" took her breath away. Some might think it grim and frightful-looking; that wasn't what she felt when she stood in it.

Enormous cragged mountains exhausted the landscape—piercing and constant, with a dark shimmer that lent an almost fantastical appearance. And above that: a purple sky. The dusky low light resembling Earth skies right after a sunset. The only thing missing was the feel of it on her skin, the smells, Tori thought. And wondered briefly if Aderus had omitted those things because they seemed entirely possible with this level of technology. Nevertheless, the simulation enveloped her. No different than if she were actually there.

It was so strange, but she felt an automatic connection to this place, that was probably thousands of light years away, if not more. It may have been her feelings for him, or something in seeing it that called to her, but the thought of this kind of beauty being destroyed enraged her. Simple as that.

"When the destroyers are ready, I want to go with you," she said firmly, embracing the impulse.

Her big Askari drew up, eyes lighting. She hadn't been sure of how he'd react, then her heart fluttered because Tori loved the way he looked at her in that moment. Loved his home, loved...him. She finally admitted. And she wanted to be with him to save it, whether or not he returned her feelings. In time, she had hope it was possible. That was enough for now.

Aderus moved closer with an appreciative hiss. Of course, her acting all valiant would get him worked up and Tori almost chuckled. But when she felt the heavy weight of his braids stir the air and claws snag her hip, that humor left her. Her heart picked up, breaths growing shallow as she stared at his torso.

A sharp peal made them both jump. Her shoulders dropped and Tori muttered under her breath once she realized what it was. She answered the comm call, Aderus still hovering over her.

"Dr. Davis? We heard you were just cleared for duty. We could really use you in the Med Ward."

"Ah, okay. Absolutely, I'll be right there," she replied, then disconnected. Her eyes flicked up to his and she swallowed as he clicked temptingly into her ear.

"They need me on the *Amendment*," she explained. Then Tori used a hand on his stomach to steady herself. She rose quickly onto her toes, watching his irises broaden right before she placed a kiss at the corner of his mouth.

Maybe she'd get him used to kissing. Maybe not, she smirked.

***

It was a little strange, as Tori tried to jump into her old work routine. The *Amendment* needed help checking on passengers and/or crew injured during the power surges, and she was happy to oblige, except that most stared blatantly at her eyes. She smiled, trying to ignore it, and successfully deflected most of the ones bold enough to ask questions. By the end of the day, though, she was worn, and realized she much preferred her time working with the Askari. Still, she put in a full shift and spoke briefly with Mina, Yin and Wells before heading back to her rooms. It'd been hard not to think of Aderus when that's all her brain seemed to want to focus on, the idea of seeing him being what ultimately got her through the day.

She took a shower, ate, then thought about how, in one way or another, he was the person she'd spent the most time with these past few weeks. When the comm interrupted them earlier, he hadn't seemed happy, and honestly, neither was she. Tori stepped away from him, taking in as much of the simulation as she could before it ended, loath to leave such beauty.

But as the evening wore on with no sign of him, her hopes fell. She sat, listening through the open access as she flipped around mindlessly on her tablet. Eventually, Tori made her way to the arboretum. It was while standing there that the idea something was off struck her. The jubilant chirping of insects and various night-time critters sounded clearly through the forest, making her recall that she seldom heard them as loudly since the Askari prowled.

She frowned, wondering what might be going on as she headed back into her rooms. Her mind began working and she was tempted to activate Henry to try to "summon" Aderus, if that's how in fact how it worked. But she was hesitant to, now that he seemed harder to control.

You're going to have to learn how eventually, her inner voice chided. *Especially now that you volunteered to help fight a war.* The thought made her stomach drop, and she made a mental note to start doing so, but only with Aderus present for help if need be.

That was the last thing she remembered before jerking awake sometime later, her neck cricking painfully from how she'd fallen asleep in the chair. The entry chime was going off and she looked over at her tablet. It was 3 a.m.

Tori struggled to get up, one foot numb from having sat on it. She thought she heard something as she spoke, accessing the outer feeds so she could see who it was. A small escort stood outside her door, soldiers among them. But before she could re-act something big moved to her left, right inside the room.

Tori met Aderus's stare, wide gold eyes rendering her immobile. He seemed to hover, as if gauging her reaction before crossing the space to tower over her chair from the side.

"Come," he rumbled down at her.

Chapter Seventeen

Tori told the group outside the entry she needed a minute and quickly used the bathroom. Obviously, something big was happening, but she didn't bother to ask what until she had herself together.

When she came out, Aderus was still there, waiting patiently, though the air felt charged.

"What's going on?" she asked, automatically switching into crisis mode. He turned as she approached him, indicating she should follow, and Tori didn't question it. They walked through the adjoining suite to enter the corridor together and he glanced down at her as they did. "Progress," he purred thickly.

Tori shivered, mostly at the way in which he'd said it: with relish. It made her heart pick up and a tingle run down her spine. The group outside her suite's entry came toward them.

"Dr. Davis? We're supposed to escort you."

The faint sound of Aderus clicking his claws registered and Tori watched him follow the others with his eyes, but he allowed them to lead. They turned down various corridors, until she finally determined they were headed to the observatory. It was a recreational area, mostly. Offering expansive views of the ship and surrounding space, but hardly no one would be there at this hour.

That was precisely the intent, she realized as they entered and Tori halted.

"Ah, good," Wells said, acknowledging her. "Dr. Davis, Representative Aderus. I think that now we can begin?"

Her eyes moved quickly about the room. Mina was there—looking a little flustered—Yin, the captain and a number of soldiers and guards. As well as some other higher-ranking individuals she didn't know. Military, by the looks of their uniforms.

But she saw quickly that humans weren't the only ones present. The room was dim, for viewing purposes, with recessed lighting at the entrance and middle. Tori had to snap her jaw shut when she realized the shifting shadows along the walls were Askari, as she glanced quickly, trying to identify them by eye color. Jadar, Krim, Vepar, Xaphan, Raum, Jinn—they were all there, and more. Pity punched her gut, followed by disapproval when she didn't see crimson among the hues.

She moved with Aderus into the room. Mina came up to her.

"Hola," she said, sounding an odd combination of sleepy and alert.

"Hey," Tori replied. "Any idea what this is all about?"

"You probably know as much as I do. Whatever it is, they didn't want us to know ahead of time. Really hush-hush."

"Alright everyone," an older gentleman in uniform said, commanding attention. "We're ready," he said, looking to Aderus, then around the room. Tori noticed that only he and Jadar stood near humans—specifically herself, and Jadar hovered, not directly next to the virologist, but close by.

The port wall faded to reveal a full panorama of half the ship, as well as a pretty impressive view of Earth where it hung in the distance. To the far right, a glimpse of the Askari vessel, where it was docked at the starboard gate, but that wasn't the focus. Directly center was the very large skeleton of a ship. It looked more alien than any Earth ship in shape, and all eyes in the room seemed focused on it. She knew it was the beginning of a hybrid destroyer, obviously. What else would it be?

Then they all watched as something moved toward the structure. It came from the starboard side, an object almost like a missile but slower. It hit the frame, but instead of exploding, there was a flash of blue light and Tori heard murmurs. She narrowed her eyes, trying to identify what was happening. Something was moving over the metal but it was hard to follow against the blackness of space. Her lips parted at the telltale shimmer of Askari technology, right before a low rumbling started along the back of the room. Soon hissing could be heard and that pretty purring that made her blush because the only other time she'd heard it was when—

Not *going there right now.*

The humans in the room turned as the space filled with sound and Tori started when Aderus joined in with a purred growl. They were all staring at the structure. She regarded it again, watching the fluid black substance move slowly along the ship's frame, emitting a faint ripple of light.

It finally occurred to her what was happening, and Tori grew still, witnessing the makings of an alien ship. The first Earth-Askara hybrid vessel, technically, but it looked like Askari technology would be a greater part. It was thrilling to behold, but for them especially, because of what it might mean.

Tori pressed her lips together, stepping close to Aderus. Giving in to the urge, she reached blindly for his hand, wrapping her fingers around two of his larger ones. The rough purring stuttered...and then long digits curled, slowly enveloping her hand. Tori started, a somewhat stunned expression on her face. His gaze was on the ship, but in a way, it felt more intimate than anything they'd shared, and her heart soared.

"How long until it's fully functional?" she questioned softly, once the hissing, growls and purrs lessened.

"Several *sols*. And more alloy," he answered.

"Which you'll be sure to get," someone interrupted from behind. "Just as soon as we get access to a few more of those suits."

Tori turned, releasing Aderus's hand. It was one of the higher-ranked men in uniform, and he was nodding to the disc at the base of her neck. She tensed at his words while Aderus clicked softly.

"I'm sure what Admiral Lewis meant to say was, there were some things we hoped to discuss before the next transport," Wells intervened smoothly as he came up beside them.

"What things would those be?" Tori said.

Steel-gray eyes took her in. "With all due respect, Dr. Davis, there are reasons you won't be a part of these negotiations."

Tori recoiled. She was aware of a faint hissing and was surprised that it came from Jadar, where he stood a few feet behind the admiral. The male's bright green eyes were locked onto the man, and she caught Mina's dazed expression as she noticed it too.

"With all due respect to you, Admiral," Tori returned calmly. "That's not something they're ready to do. And as I can personally attest, I don't think we're ready to handle. I'm still learning to control it myself."

"We have operatives that are highly trained, both physically and mentally, to be able to handle such things, Doctor," he said, staring her down. "We'd be very careful who we gave that kind of technology to. Anything less, would be just plain stupid," he finished, looking at Aderus.

Tori glared at the backhanded insult, right before the situation quickly devolved. Aderus reacted, pressing forward with a deep hiss as guards on either side of the admiral angled their weapons. Suddenly there were sides—humans versus Askari.

Warning clicks and hisses surrounded them as the other soldiers in the room formed a circle. "Let's all just take a breath!" Wells said, raising his hands in a placating gesture. But the plea fell on deaf ears when Xaphan reached out and snatched a weapon away from one of the men who was pointing it at him. Someone fired off a taser round, and the whole room erupted into chaos.

Aderus and Jadar leapt forward, and Tori was terrified as she saw them slam into two other Askari before realizing they were trying to deflect the aggression onto themselves. She rushed toward them, determined to stop more shots from being fired in turn, as she threw herself in front of the soldiers.

"Get outta the way!" one of them shouted over the hissing snarls behind her.

"Put your damn weapons down!" she shot back, glancing quickly over her shoulder. The one Aderus was holding surged forward, and Tori ducked when a limb came flying near her head. Her fingers automatically went to the disc at the base of her neck, but froze with sudden indecision.

Her heart raced as she turned back, looking into the middle of the room. Wells was on his comm, the admiral was barking orders. If she activated Henry now, they'd all see it. They'd all know what it was capable of and she doubted she'd be able to control it. Everyone would be affected—what if she killed people? As her head panned to the side, she saw Askari watched her, a few with flashing teeth. One even started for her.

Tori lowered her fingers, managing to find Aderus's gaze just as he pushed away from the fray. His eyes flicked quickly between her face and her hand where it dropped from her neck and he hissed deeply, focusing on something behind her. Tori *oomphed* as the breath was knocked from her body in the next instant. She half expected it to be the Askari she'd seen moving for her, but the shoulder against her stomach felt human. The last sight she saw as she strained her back, trying to keep upright while being carted off, was someone pointing a gun at Aderus.

"*No!*" she shouted, reaching for him.

Chapter Eighteen

Tori paced her quarters, hanging on to her composure by a thread. They'd completely evacuated the observation room, but she had no idea what happened yet, if Aderus was okay. That's all she wanted to know; the rest could be dealt with, she told herself.

They'd sequestered her here, two guards stationed at the entry. Tori tried comm-ing Wells but couldn't get through. Mina wasn't answering either. She even attempted to speak with the men in the corridor, with no luck.

The sound of parting doors drew her to a halt. She rushed into the adjoining suite, just in time to see Aderus stalking into the room and a hand went to her mouth.

"Oh, thank goodness," she mumbled, freezing in her steps. "Are you alright? What happened?" she said, looking him over quickly. He didn't seem to be injured, which let her relax slightly.

Aderus pinned her with a glare and advanced, tresses out. "You wouldn't wear the *havat*," he growled, and she stumbled a step, confused as to why he'd be upset.

"Yes, and you know why," she told him.

He kept coming, until Tori felt the arm of an over-sized chair against her legs and her hands flew to grip his forearm to keep from tumbling backward. Then his snout was in her hair, nudging the side of her head. Claws pricked the sensitive skin of one butt cheek and she yelped. She quickly deduced he wasn't angry, and her breaths quickened. Aderus's passionate assault ignited an answering fire in her, but Tori froze, focusing on what he'd said.

Wait... He'd *wanted* her to activate Henry? Aderus knew she couldn't control it, but he'd been more concerned for her protection than for everyone else in that room?

The thought set her aflame with what it implied, as Tori slumped awkwardly across the chair's arm and back under the weight of her emotions. Aderus followed with a rasping hiss, claws scraping the cushions. There was nothing graceful about it—he practically fell on her trying to maneuver his limbs over and around the piece of furniture, the sight probably comical. But Tori was all seriousness as she reached for him, one hand working hard to free a leg from her scrub bottoms. She was frantic, caught up in their combined fervor.

Aderus hissed when her fingers brushed his groin, her other hand holding tight to the back of his arm for balance. One of his legs slipped along her inner thigh and Tori watched his *havat* begin to recede up his body, panting slightly. Lithe arms braced to the right and above her, entrapping her against the cushions, and when he growled her eyes shot to his. She searched the golden orbs, wanting him to know how she felt.

"Aderus—" Her voice caught at the sensation of wetness against her fingers. He rasped, tresses falling into her face.

"I love you," Tori blurted, latching one leg to his hip so that she could grasp his jaw. He jerked at the touch, and his eyes locked onto hers.

"Do you know what that means?" she murmured, going still. "It means that I care for you deeply. And you are the only one I want to do *this* with." Her fingers slicked through his folds to demonstrate her meaning. Aderus hissed, the thing within his body pushing restlessly, and Tori swallowed. She'd tried to put it in a way he would understand, blazing eyes regarding her as she took the final step off a terrifying ledge.

"Do Askari have such a word?"

No matter what he said, she would *not* let it gut her, she thought, breaths turning shallow. A rolling click passed between them.

"No word," he grated, eyes moving over her face, and she flinched, fingers going slack.

"I see," she said dully, turning her head to the side. Her lip trembled.

Keep it together, do not *cry,* she ordered herself.

Tori jerked when she felt a hot gust against her neck and an unexpected sound overwhelmed her senses. It was the purring hum, embellished with deliberate dips and rises. He was...singing, she realized. That was the only way to describe it.

No word.

Tori's breath caught. A half laugh, half sob escaping her as roughened fingers caressed her jaw.

He was singing, to her.

Her muscles spasmed as something strong and wet meandered up one thigh and suddenly she was panting, latching on to Aderus's waist and back while his body pressed her further into the cushions. She moaned when it found her center, reaching up to grip his nape while her legs slid desperately along his hips. A snarl peppered his humming, along with the tearing of fabric.

She cried out as the tip of him found her clit and Tori's scalp tingled from his jaw against her temple, the vibrations flowing into her. She didn't need much foreplay, wound tight as she was. So, when he teased, then pushed his way into her, the deep stretching sensation was all it took. Tori's limbs locked around him, every muscle clenching helplessly with sharp release...

***

Aderus dug his claws into the soft spongy material, letting his *krhunes* warble in a way expressive of his thoughts and emotions. There was no word for what Tori described, but his kind sometimes communicated profound feeling with sound, or what Earthers would call *song*. When he'd seen her purposefully sacrifice herself for the sake of what she knew mattered to him, whatever he'd felt before erupted into something hot and violent. Aderus kept seeing her face when she told him she wanted to fight for his world, and it was as if the knowing in him, one he now recognized revolved around her, besieged him.

He'd watched her being carried away. Jadar, Krim and Vepar helping to keep the others distracted while the diplomat Wells handled the humans. Working with them was proving difficult, full of conflict. But Earth and Askara's paths were now the same, and what Tori had just done helped him to see it.

Aderus growled as his *pvost* slid into her, focusing on how she'd said he was the only one she wanted to breed. And when she wrapped herself around his body, it didn't bother him much. He bred her until she pushed him away, spilling into her tight cavern more than once. The pleasure-pain left him spent and slightly weak, as he untangled his limbs from the human contraption, watching Tori's eyes flutter where she lay.

"Stay," she muttered, small, blunt fingers grabbing his lightly. Aderus allowed it, watching her nod into sleep. Humans slept a lot, and he wondered briefly what it would be like, spending twice as much time defenseless. Likely another reason they shared living space so readily. Curiously, he found the idea no longer repelled him—as long as it was Tori—and being so close to the Earthscape appealed to his inner urges.

He rose slowly, noting her half-exposed flesh. A soft hiss escaped him as Aderus reached for the disc of her *havat*. He didn't feel the need to move her if he was going to stay and explore...but the covering would cleanse and warm her skin, and it made him feel better to see it over her.

Chapter Nineteen
...a few days later

"Nope, I told you," Tori said, shaking her head.

"I can't believe you can't even give me one measly detail. *Other than* it's a guy," Liv grumped. Her best friend had been shocked, then ecstatic when Tori finally confessed she was rooming with someone. But Liv's mood quickly soured when she found that was the only piece of information Tori could divulge.

"He's gotta be pretty special if you agreed to let him into your neurotic little world," Liv said, pinching her bottom lip.

"Shut up," she quipped.

"And someone with super-advanced clearance, considering everything you've been going through... Please tell me he's got stripes. Gods, I love a man in uniform."

"You'll find out soon enough."

Likely any day now, after the near catastrophe in the observatory. The powers that be had labeled Liv's proposal and others like it of the highest priority—anything to help with relations. Which ultimately boiled down to, in Liv's case, attempting to work with the most reticent Askari.

Things with her own surly alien, on the other hand, were going amazingly well, she mused. It was as if there'd been a whole part of her life Tori never realized was missing and the more time she spent with Aderus, the more she wondered how she ever could have thought he didn't, or couldn't, have serious feelings for her.

Things were still quite new, of course. So, she was loath to label anything yet. But it was in his actions. The little changes she saw, and the way he was slowly indulging her needs, as long as she was clear about them. Tori knew Askari didn't have the same requirements for words and affection as humans did. It merely made the times they did share those things more special, and Tori liked to think she was drawing out some long-dormant part of him. As if the potential was there, they just had to discover it.

Like when she'd awoken after he'd sung to her and Aderus was there, sitting quietly next to her.

His kind didn't need as much rest, she'd learned, and night was when they prowled the arboretum. Whenever he seemed anxious or irritated, it's where he sought to be, and it reminded Tori of their wildness. That the terrain was alien didn't matter, apparently. Most were just glad to indulge their instincts, and some even seemed to like the forest, which was completely different from the simulation she'd seen.

Their world had been beautiful, stunningly different. But only afterward did Tori realize she'd seen nothing that resembled vegetation. As in, absolutely none. No wonder he'd sneered at her trail bar the first time. Theirs was a completely different kind of biological system.

The last few days had seen some major developments, however, as Tori began training with Henry. It was the compromise they'd come to in order to keep the transports coming: she agreed to monitored sessions—demonstrations of its abilities and ways to harness them—with the intent to train a very select few humans to use them in the coming war for Askara. Because no matter how Earth governments tried to play it planet-side, that's exactly what was coming, and the thought was sobering.

The Askari were mostly on board with it. At least one usually sat-in, a.k.a. hovered stoically in the background, while she worked. Tori knew some saw it as the only way to get what they needed, but that's how alliances worked sometimes.

Aderus often appeared and she always felt a little thrill when he was there. Every time she saw him, she fell a little harder and it both surprised and delighted her how often he'd seek her out. To be honest, Tori thought of and craved seeing him just as often. But she knew their relationship was still very strange for everyone and not particularly accepted, so she tried not to advertise it. Really though, it was no one's damn business.

Today, Henry was being particularly fussy.

"Come on, buddy, don't give me a hard time," she mumbled down at him, running her hands lightly over the dark sleeves. He wasn't responding to her mental commands. Or when he did it was exaggerated, the reaction almost explosive.

Tori looked up, spotting Aderus through the transparent barrier, golden gaze raking her from where he stood near the wall.

The room was a lot like the one she woke in after her eyes changed, except larger and completely reinforced to handle the energy surges. The lighting was dim, for both precautionary and observation purposes; Henry loved to put on a show. The last couple days she'd been dealing with a return of her earlier symptoms, though, and he'd become much harder to control. It started with the strange drops in pitch. Which Tori now knew accompanied an enhanced ability to hear super-low frequency sounds once she realized the noises she heard came from Aderus and the others.

Honestly, it was a relief to understand what'd been happening, and definitely shed new light on those "silent" conversations she witnessed. Then came the hot flashes this morning. As if she didn't have enough to look forward to every month, being someone of the female persuasion. Now it seemed her altered genes chose around the same time to make themselves known.

Tori rubbed her forehead, looking to Aderus with an "I give up" expression. She watched him click his claws and move from the wall, approaching the sealed entry doors. Most of them were on the other side of the ship during the day, where the new destroyers were increasing in number.

"I tried the things you told me," she said when he entered. Nostrils flaring as he loomed close and thick braids grazed her shoulders. It was their own version of intimacy. She was gradually getting him used to affectionate touches while he would nudge and hover, a lot more subdued than when he was aroused.

"Your scent is changed," he growled with an interested click, and Tori felt her cheeks heat. She knew that sound.

"Yeah, same as before. It's my hormones. And um, we have an audience," she said when he rooted against her ponytail, trying to keep said hormones in check. She knew it was why he'd been so fiery last night. So had she, if she were honest.

"Stop, and try later," he rumbled. Holding her gaze as he moved back. Krim stood passively in the corner of the observation area, and she had to bite her lip when Aderus snapped at him on the way out.

By the time she took a break, Tori decided to call it quits. When she allowed herself to think of the importance of what she was doing, it was a lot of pressure and he was right: sometimes it was good to step away.

She headed back to their shared quarters, retracting Henry to shower and then throw on something comfortable. She'd gotten into a routine the last few nights, of eating a little something when she got in that would hold her until later, when she liked to join him in the arboretum. Sometimes he'd enter the rooms first, and Tori kept an ear out as she watched a vid on her tablet; turning her head into the cushion as she munched on a snack. It smelled like him.

The adjoining access was kept open, so he could feel he still had his own space, should he need it. Getting Aderus to use the beds, however, was another story. Apparently, they were too soft and 'suffocating'. More than once she'd woken on the floor or in a chair after he'd worn her out because he usually kept on going until she told him to stop. Only now he was around afterward. Sometimes prowling the other rooms, or often crouched or seated quietly nearby. His eyes would open as soon as she stirred and Tori noticed he seemed to rest a lot, rather than actually sleep. When she was really tired, she made her way to a bed. But a couple times she'd woken there, both surprised and touched that he'd carried her.

Tori finished her snack. The vid wasn't really holding her interest, so she switched to some music, nodding along as she waited for him. It made her wonder if his kind danced, and the thought made her snicker until she recalled the way Aderus had moved through the trees night before last.

The entry chime went off, interrupting the image and Tori looked up, accessing the outer feeds. It was Mina. Tori met her at the door.

"Hey. Can we talk?" The virologist seemed off.

Tori's guard went up. "What's wrong? What happened?" she muttered, ushering her inside.

"No, no. It's nothing like that." Mina stopped, brown eyes darting around the room through the lenses of her glasses. "Is Aderus here?"

"Not right now."

"Good. Because, I could use your advice. *And* I have news."

"Okay. Sure," Tori frowned, gesturing for her to sit but Mina stayed where she was. "I need something cold. You want anything?"

"I'm fine, thanks," The virologist replied, watching her move into the kitchen. "Hot flashes?"

"They're not as bad as before." Tori noticed Mina was looking at her hands. She held one up as she came around the counter.

"Nothing yet. It's around that time of the month though. I've also been meaning to thank you," Tori said, stopping. "For taking the blame on the breach when we were chased onto the ship. You didn't have to do that. It's long past due, but I kept forgetting." Her face shown her sincerity.

"*De nada,*" the other woman waved her off sheepishly. "It was nothing, and you had enough you were dealing with. Have you noticed anything different?" Mina asked. She sat, but only once Tori lowered into a chair herself.

"No. My scent changes, the Askari aspect becomes more pronounced. Aderus confirmed it this morning. It drives them a little crazy."

Mina leaned close. "You do smell different, now that you mention it. Musky, or...smoky?" she said, sniffing delicately as she pulled out her tablet. Presumably to make note of it. "It's very slight though."

"Then I wasn't just imagining it," Tori mumbled, turning her nose into her shoulder. "You're the first human to say so—wow, that sounds weird. As long as I'm wearing Henry the others keep their distance."

"Henry?" Mina said, looking confused.

"It's what I call the covering." Tori clarified, not embarrassed in the least.

The virologist's expression cleared then turned serious. "Em, speaking of, we got the results from your germline analysis." She paused. "And the changes to your DNA are inclusive of your eggs."

Tori froze, cold creeping over her skin. "What are you saying?"

"As it stands, you can't become pregnant—humans and Askari are still two very different species. But..." Mina's eyes were wide, seemingly at a loss for words, and Tori understood why.

"If I have children, I'd pass the changes on to them," she finished. Essentially, her children wouldn't be fully human. Tori had been trying to prepare herself for the scenario because she'd known about the tests. But it didn't stave the swell of emotion in that moment.

"Our superiors want you on something, just in case," Mina murmured.

"Right. I'll take care of it," Tori replied, gaze slightly unfocused. She'd never had any intention of having children. Kids were great, but Tori had long ago accepted she wasn't mother material. Her career was her life, she was happy with it that way. But now it made her wonder—had Aderus sired children? She'd been so caught up with the past few weeks, she hadn't asked him about those things yet. Their relationship was still new and actually going well; Tori hadn't wanted to intentionally stir the pot. It reminded her that he had a whole other life before that she often forgot about.

"They're also moving forward with the pilot program," Mina said, pulling her away again and Tori's gaze shot to her.

"Are you serious?"

From her expression, the virologist was completely serious. "The benefits outweigh the costs. Per the governments, we have to put everything we can into this. Because if we get there and fail then what's to keep those monsters from coming after Earth?" There was a pause. "Did Aderus show you what they look like yet?"

Tori shook her head, knowing she was right, and a shiver ran down her spine.

Mina looked horrified. "*Dios, chica*, you don't want to know."

"Participation is voluntary," she continued. "Operatives will be kept on multiple forms of birth control. At least they'll know what they're getting into. You didn't."

"Yeah, but. I don't regret anything," Tori blinked, realizing as she said it that it was true.

"There's nothing you would, do different? Even knowing what I just told you?" Mina asked, watching her quietly.

"Absolutely not," Tori said. "I love Aderus. I know that's probably hard for you to understand because they seem so different, but—"

"It's not. It's not so hard," Mina interrupted, looking down. She blew out a breath. "*Mierda*, maybe I do need a drink." Tori's brows went up. There weren't many things Mina could be seeking her out for advice on. "So, how—how *different* do you mean?"

A slow grin spread across Tori's face. "Oh, boy. Let me get you that drink first."

Chapter Twenty

Aderus entered their shared living space and paused. Tori was through the open access; he could scent her, lifting his snout as he clicked softly. There was another scent too, the female with the crooked tresses. He'd seen her often around Jadar.

When he approached, however, Tori was alone. Bent over the electronic slab she called a *tablet*. Humans interacted with them often, almost as often as with each other, and she'd shown him the distractions it contained. Aderus much preferred roaming the Earthscape, or resting quietly, but it was clear her kind still hadn't learned how to integrate technology with reality yet.

He moved behind her, staring briefly at the strange, small figures while Tori hummed, completely immersed. The sound wasn't as rich and complex as what his own throat could produce but he liked listening to it all the same, attention shifting to her tresses.

That she hadn't sensed him spoke to how oblivious Earthers could be, and when Aderus thought of her joining in the fight for Askara, it made him uneasy. He would never tell her, but it was the reason he was present while she worked with the *havat*... Second to the fact that he craved the sight of her. When they'd first met such notions seemed impossible, but males sought Askari females just as often when they cycled, he reasoned. Humans were merely more receptive, and also more docile. It made him consider the ways in which their cultures might have been closer, if those factors were the same.

157

Her scent rose then, enveloping him. Aderus growled softly as he took it in.

Tori started, whipping around. She looked fearful and grabbed her chest before a smile showed her flat white teeth.

"You're gonna give me a heart attack one of these days, you know that?"

He watched as she rose, eyes roving her body when she lifted her arms to stretch. "Mina was here. Though you probably smell her."

He *snikted* in answer, studying her. "You are well?" Aderus knew the other female monitored her.

"Yeah." The way she said it sounded odd. It made him want to ask again. "Oh! I want to show you something."

Tori's smile returned and she walked hurriedly through the access, into the uncluttered rooms that he preferred. Aderus followed, watching her enter the *bedroom* and look back at him.

"I ditched the sheets and blankets and adjusted the mattress to the firmest setting, see?"

She bent over, bouncing her weight on her hands as she touched the platform. "I thought it'd appeal to you more this way," she said, looking over her shoulder. Aderus had stopped just outside the space and watched her through the entrance. He still had little interest in human *beds*, but the way she was bent made his eyes flare and a faint hiss escape him as his attention fixed on her rear.

Tori straightened with a puff of breath. "I swear, you have such a one-track mind." The sounds she made were those of amusement, despite her reaction, and Aderus found himself appreciating the thought behind what she'd done. Earthers' fascination with how they slept still made no sense. As long as the space was safe, preferably hidden, what did it matter what one laid upon? Aderus noticed she did sleep better on them though, which is why he had moved her more than once when he sensed she was overly tired...half expecting her to wake and slap him away, as she'd hung limp in his arms, but she hadn't.

"I can see you're still not sold," she said, sticking her lips out.

His gaze flicked to the platform. "It looks, less unpleasant."

He could give her that, at least. For her efforts. What had she termed it? Being courteous. Tori laughed and reached to squeeze his fingers as she passed. Aderus brayed, shifting closer but she kept going toward the access to the Earthscape. He'd grown increasingly used to her small touches, even when others stared, both human and Askari alike.

When the access opened, admitting a gush of warm air, Aderus's nostrils flared and he straightened. He watched Tori step onto the dusty loam and followed, coming up behind her as his senses soaked in the surroundings. He looked forward to this time of day, when they'd enter together as the too bright sun set.

Aderus moved around her, advancing down the path. He didn't have to turn to know Tori trailed him, ears pricking at the sound of her steps. He sensed more than one Askari nearby and slowed, clicking low.

"You should don your *havat*, others are close."

He didn't like her being without it, especially when her scent was as enticing. Seeing its glow ensured the others left her alone.

"Oh, really? Who?" she asked brightly.

It seemed a source of entertainment for her, that he could name them by scent. Aderus's tresses bristled, and he had to remind himself it was curiosity. Her attention on other males still provoked displeasure but that was their nature.

His chin lifted. "Xaphan, Vepar, Jinn...Braxas," he growled.

He led them off the path, away from prying human devices, and stopped twice to let her catch him. Satisfied when he saw a contrasting darkness against her skin. Aderus snatched a *bug* from the air as he waited, enjoying the pleasant crunch and squish of it in his mouth.

Tori shielded her eyes as she approached. "Ugh. Can you *not* do that when I'm around? I kiss that mouth. You're giving me nightmares."

It obviously disgusted her, which he found amusing. Everything he ate repulsed her and Aderus loosed a sharp snort. Nearly everything humans ate repulsed him too. Especially the things that came from their food generators.

The light continued to fade as they moved beneath the *trees*, until Aderus froze, feeling her brush up against him from behind. He hissed faintly, splaying his claws to indicate she still. His ears were erect as he looked above them, sensing movement.

Aderus willed his havat to part around his feet and readied to jump. The small pelted creature never stood a chance as he scaled the *tree*, hearing the animal's keen cry of alarm a moment before his claws found it. He dug his feet hard into the crumbling *bark* to hold his weight and made quick work of the morsel. Then looked down before he dropped, to gauge where Tori was.

The first time he'd done this, it was *her* cry of alarm he'd heard. Earthers were sensitive that way, he remembered. They didn't like to witness death, and most did not feel the need to hunt and kill their food. Now she closed her eyes and covered her ears whenever he readied to attack.

Aderus landed a short distance from her, moving his tongue over his lips and claws, trying to get every trace he could before she opened her eyes. The pelted creatures seemed to bother her more, and though he found her distress at something so natural vexing, he also didn't like to see her upset. Aderus moved close, until she sensed and responded to his presence.

One shining blue eye peaked up at him. "Are you done?" She'd dropped to her haunches while she waited and Aderus followed suit, lowering slowly into a crouch opposite her. He could sense the reaching *tree trunk* along his back.

"Yes," he rumbled.

Her hands dropped from her ears. "There must be something wrong with me, because despite what I know you just did, I still find you sexy," she said, lips twitching. Then the teasing twist to them fell and the air between them thickened.

"Aderus, Mina told me something today," she said, gaze holding his. "It doesn't really affect us, but...I have to know. Do you have children?"

Aderus's spines rippled as he sensed her unease. He didn't know what answer she was expecting; breeding produced offspring, that was its purpose. Except not always with humans.

Aderus looked away, considering the question. He was sure he had sired younglings, though it was uncertain whether they still lived. "It is likely."

Tori blinked. "You don't know?"

His gaze locked onto her bright blue orbs again, their likeness to a *dahvhrin's* tresses unsettling.

"It is not a male's place to know or care for his progeny. A harboring female wouldn't allow it."

"That seems—cruel."

He shifted, claws scraping the ground. Perhaps to her, it would, because humans cared for, even lived with their young. Aderus didn't understand those inclinations but he'd often been curious. He wondered what his progeny would look like, if they shared his traits. If they were fierce, like some of the females he'd bred.

"Males can care for newly born young. If the female dies, and the offspring is his own. But Askari young are very instinctual. They would not stay with either parent long."

"Would you know them if you saw them?" Tori asked softly, as if she had read his mind, and his eyes moved sharply between her own.

When Aderus had first come to know her, speaking like this made him guarded, even snappish. And when deeper feelings for her began to emerge, he hadn't known how to manage them. Especially as he dealt with the humans, battling for patience while his own people hovered on the edge of extinction. So, he'd closed himself off, relying heavily on instinct to guide him.

The past several *sols*, however, things with Earth governments had changed. Tori helped him to realize that perhaps what stood most in the way of saving their home was themselves, and their approach to dealing with her people. Conflict would arise, as they were now well versed. But despite, or perhaps because of it, relations with the humans were evolving into something the likes of which they'd never experienced... And it was the same with what Aderus felt for her. That he could tell her things he rarely, if ever, spoke of with anyone and Tori tried not to judge him. Even when they were completely different from what she knew.

"I do not know," he finally answered. Watching as she looked down and fiddled with the short springing brush around her legs. "You have birthed young?"

Her head jerked up; eyes wide. "Gods, no! You would have known before now if that were the case."

He clicked softly, but she offered an explanation before he could wonder. "Raising human children is a lifetime commitment," she smiled strangely. "I decided a long time ago that wasn't what I wanted. Kind of makes me wonder about Askari children though."

"They are smaller, just as fierce," he growled, recalling a time he'd come across a young female, just set out from her *gr-rhlyen*. She'd swiped at him when he came close while digging for *rukhhal*. Though it was natural, something about the sight of her wandering the war-ravaged valleys had bothered him, and one of his blunted tresses still bore her scar.

"I can imagine," she huffed. Aderus's ear flicked as he heard a sound and when he glanced back Tori was looking to the sky. There was a slight opening in the cover above them where stars were visible.

"Mina also said she'd seen the *Maekhurz...*"

Aderus bit back the snarl that threatened at the mere mention of their name.

"When you are ready, I will show you," he rumbled. Thinking of the progress she'd made with the *havat*. Other than the times her symptoms interfered, Tori showed great ability and it helped stave his restlessness as they waited for more battle vessels to form. With hope, it would not be much longer. Earth had increased their transports and the rate at which things were now progressing left him feeling more assured than he could remember. At the same time, he worried over their readiness, human readiness, at the battle to come.

"There's Orion," she said, pointing to the sky. "And the big dipper."

Aderus knew what she was doing. When she sensed him growing agitated, she would attempt to distract him. He'd done the same with her before, and considering the dark direction of his thoughts, he let her.

"They're constellations. Groupings of stars that we name to help us identify them," she explained. "All the constellations have stories."

"What stories?" he rumbled, seeking more of the soft lilt of her voice.

Her face tipped toward him. "Oh, well…"

Aderus felt his muscles loosen as she lulled him with human myths and legends, and when his feet began to cramp in their position beneath him, he stretched out his legs, leaning back against the hard plant. His ears stayed erect, while his eyes would follow any nearby sound, but her stories must have relaxed him enough that he drifted. Next Aderus knew he was waking with a startled hiss, baring both rows of teeth at the feel of something unknown brushing his foot. Tori was stretched across the ground at his feet, regarding him quietly.

"I'm glad to see you enjoy my story-telling."

He calmed when he saw it was her, watching as she ran a finger lightly along the underside of his foot. The touch tickled and his foot curled, enclosing her much smaller hand completely within his grasp, along with part of her arm.

Tori stilled, seemingly content to feel their skin touch. Then she began to squirm. Twisting her body in a way that confused him until he realized she was slipping out of the Earth clothes.

Aderus released her hand, chin lifting to test her scent with a deep rolling click and he started when she rose onto her hands and knees. His eyes lit, fingers curling eagerly into the ground. But pale digits grasped his thigh.

"Stay like that. Please?"

His mind disagreed. It wanted her stretched beneath him so that he could feel her soft flesh against his plated chest, but as always, his body heeded her words...at least until their breeding incensed him enough that instinct ruled over them both.

The rumble he exuded cut short when she swung a leg over his hips, balancing herself upon his bulge. The pressure caused discomfort and Aderus hissed; digging the claws of all four limbs into the loam before he jerked his legs up, ceasing her movements. Then he watched her *havat* retract up her body, eyes brightening as he devoured her slight form.

"I have a surprise. I waxed," she said, looking between them.

Aderus didn't know what she was talking about until he followed her gaze. Noticing the soft bristles that usually covered her modest folds were gone. The stab of lust that hit him once he realized what it allowed made him snarl and his *havat* began to retract without his knowing; responding to some deeper command as his conscious mind fixed on the vision of her sat upon his open folds.

His muscles tightened in anticipation, *vryll* already parted beneath what still covered his groin and he felt Tori quiver. Her eyes were wide as they locked with his, and she began to pant. Aderus tried to remember if she had asked him about it, or that she might have guessed he was sensitive there by his reactions to her touches, but the feel of her soft, smooth flesh against him as the material pulled between them incensed him. Tori's legs spasmed and she moaned at the contact, head dropping forward onto his chest. She began to move almost instantly, rocking her hips against his slick membranes and Aderus had to fight not to push her to the ground.

He snarled again, unleashing a harsh series of clicks and shut his eyes briefly as his *pvost* whipped insistently within his body. Cold ran down his spine as he fought to contain it.

"Oh boy. This is *way* more intense than I thought. Hold on, baby. I'm almost there," Tori breathed.

He felt her soft fingers along the side of his face and neck, as Aderus's tresses flattened with the effort to restrain himself. He vaguely recognized the name Tori had begun calling him frequently when excited and at the sound of her low cry, he let go.

His tresses puffed, shrouding them both as his *pvost* broke free to find her and he reached to frame her jaw. Dust kicked between them from the force of his movements, but Aderus snorted it away. Too focused on watching Tori react as his eager appendage found its way inside while her body continued to convulse. Her eyes shot open, locking with his own, and *krhunes* erupted from his chest and throat without him trying. Warbling prettily, as she said.

Tori turned into his fingers, pushing them toward her mouth, *kissing* and licking him. Then her blunt teeth bit down sharply. Aderus snapped his jaw at the sensation. She couldn't break the skin, but it was enough to trigger his release and more dust billowed when he locked her hips to his tightly with his other hand, claws curling helplessly into her delicate flesh.

The things she made him feel still amazed him. Aderus reflected afterward with Tori slumped against him, nearly asleep by the sound of her breathing. They were still connected, and his *pvost* twitched questioningly but he would not breed her while she rested. He didn't mind the way she lay, and the fact she chose to stay joined spoke further to how thoroughly she accepted him. Aderus couldn't ever remember feeling as satisfied, he thought.

A sudden lull in the calls around them caused his skin to tighten. Aderus tensed, pulling from her with a low hiss as he turned into the darkness. But his snout told him all he needed to know.

Tori jostled against his chest when he rose, shelving her haunches with one arm as her legs dangled astride his hips. Then he paused, clicking measuredly with warning into the brush. He made their way back to the path...feeling for Tori's *havat* as he willed his own down his body while they went.

When he reached their rooms, he considered what she'd shown him and set her upon the less unpleasant *bed*. Her fine tresses flowed through his claws, and he stood playing with them for a time before he huffed, thinking of things she told him in the Earthscape.

Aderus studied her, resting peacefully on the platform.

The little Earther pushed him; changed him in ways he was still grasping to understand, and would continue to do so, he was sure. But he no longer thought of a reality where they hadn't jumped through into this world, because he didn't want to imagine one without her.

He turned, making sure to speak the command to close the room's access. Aderus felt better knowing she was hidden securely behind it until he returned. Then he headed back into the Earthscape, letting his snout guide him as he retraced his steps.

Not for the first time, he wondered how his people would react when they came with a force of Earthers and ships. *If* they could take back their world. The sizable fleet that was now forming in the space around them sparked fire in his veins, even as Tori pulled at his thoughts once more.

He worried if he could protect her, how other Askari might treat her when they made contact and decided it did not matter. He wouldn't let anything harm her while he still breathed and the *khurzha* was already her own force with what she had mastered of their technology. With any luck, she could train other humans to do the same, and soon.

Aderus stopped then, as the scent he sought found him. He listened carefully to his surroundings for any sign of movement, and when he heard the whisper of some small creature near his feet, he struck; trapping it with his claws and holding it prisoner while it squirmed. Having chosen the offering, he set off for his intended target.

Aderus heard the male's deep clicking before he saw him: bright red eyes coming into view as he moved between two *trees*. The *palkriv* was crouched, prepared to attack while he tracked Aderus's movements with a baited hiss. Aderus stared at him. The male was mostly covered by his *havat* but the contrast, where it met bare skin, reminded him very much of Tori.

He held up the offering, watching the male's gaze lock onto it as it wriggled. Wary eyes looked between him and the creature, then blinked.

Aderus tossed it to him. Staying only long enough to watch him catch it as the animal emitted a high-pitched squeal of distress. The gesture didn't require words and he could count on one hand the number of times he'd hunted for another. It wasn't many. The more he'd thought about what Tori said, however, the more it began to disturb him, how the male was treated. She was right—this was not Askara. And those things had no relevance here.

From the look on the *palkriv's* face, it was the first time he'd been afforded the kindness.

Epilogue

"I'm sorry, but I don't understand what you mean. Dr. Davis implied you'd be willing to work with us on the food printers. We assumed you could use your technology to upgrade ours. Or bridge the gap or something," Wells said, the space above his eyes wrinkling.

Jadar blinked his second eyelids patiently. He knew he was the more amenable among them, but this human could test even the most tolerant dispositions. Vepar stood to his right, with Mina next to Wells. He focused briefly on the female's fine, curling tresses. She was watching Vepar now try to explain to the ambassador what would need to happen to convert the human ship.

Askari technology could not simply integrate with other forms of engineering, that was not how it worked. Rather, it consumed them. Absorbed other energy and matter to become part of itself. If Earth governments wanted Askari technology in their vessels, the vessels had to *become* Askari. Evidently, it was a difficult concept for them to accept.

What was vital, however, was what it could afford them: a greater fighting force, and vessels that were more quickly formed. Because the sense of urgency that had finally pervaded the humans only added to their angst and Jadar could feel it, riling his normally controlled nature.

Mina met his eyes, seeming agitated.

They had been working to try and decipher the reasons behind why their technology responded to human biology the way it had, but some Earthers were to wear the *havats* regardless—in an attempt to balance their kinds' weakness and hopefully harness the same ability Tori had. While Jadar rejected Xaphan's idea at first, the Earther had impressed him with her persistence and almost obsessive way she stalked him. And he wasn't treated to female attention often, even if she was alien.

"...There are thousands of people aboard this ship. We'd have to arrange an evacuation," he heard Wells say. Vepar had at least communicated the point.

"Our technology knows the difference between living and nonliving matter," Jadar supplied.

"Apparently not," Wells said. "Seeing as it altered Dr. Davis's very DNA."

Jadar flared his nostrils, looking to the side as he clicked his teeth. The bonding that took place with a *havat* was different, but the diplomat was already skeptical.

"That was different, though," Mina spoke, and his sharp gaze cut back to her. "Dr. Davis was able to work aboard their vessel without an issue."

"I haven't forgotten your less than stellar handling of a serious breach in protocol, Dr. Perez, so you'll excuse me if I'm a little reticent to heed your professional opinion."

Jadar watched as Mina pressed her lips together and his spines stiffened at the increase in tension.

"...But. I will relay what you've said to Earth governments," he said, looking between them. "And if it's what they decide then we'll get started immediately. Thank you, for taking time from your work. I'll let you get back to it."

They watched the male walk away and Vepar made a sound to voice his angst before he too turned and left.

"*Right,*" Jadar heard her rumble softly in *Spanish*. She switched between the two human languages often, and the way in which their technology could bridge sound with thought enabled him to understand either easily. Though he recognized they were different. It was, in truth, something he'd been considering—whether the changes to Tori's makeup could afford her brain the same ability. If so, she would be able to understand them. But that could have its disadvantages.

Mina began to fidget curiously. "I was going to take a break, maybe walk the arboretum. Would you like to join me?"

At her mention of the Earthscape, his eyes flared. Unlike the others, Jadar found little time to indulge aboard the human ship and couldn't deny the appeal of what she said. Instead he clicked, drawing up while his tresses lifted. Mina's loam-colored eyes widened behind the dark lines that framed them.

She appeared uneasy, he measured, maybe even intimidated. Jadar had seen little sign of it before. Females his own kind paid him less mind precisely for that reason. But the thought that Mina, a human, might view him otherwise because of the mere differences in their bodies suddenly intrigued him.

Almost as much as her offer to prowl the Earthscape.

Author's Note

Hello again everyone! I sincerely hope you enjoyed Part II of Tori and Aderus's story ☺

In writing this book, I've discovered my approach to romance is from the perspective that relationships never really end, do they? Instead, they culminate in two people realizing their deep feelings of love, affection and/or commitment to one another and the rest is an adventure I think is better left a bit open-ended. All the more satisfying for its element of "realness"...that's definitely me lol, keep'n it real.

As for Tori and Aderus, fear not! We will continue to see snippets/appearances from them throughout the rest of the series, but up next? Mina and Jadar's story; in case you hadn't guessed. I've already started developing things between these two and can tell you I am SO excited for this book (yes, I'm still playing with the title). All I can say is: questions are answered, and things go galactic *eyebrow wag*. Expect a release Spring-ish 2020, with a cover reveal after the new year :D

As always, I'd love to hear from you! Connect with me on Facebook (JMLinkAuthor), Twitter (@linktojm) or my blog https://jmlinkblog.blogspot.com. You can subscribe to my Mailing List, Linked to JM, for emails on releases, promos and special giveaways via my Facebook page or blog. And if you enjoyed *Earth*, please, please leave a review. I never realized as a reader how important they are, but, well, it's true. And I read every one <3

Love and hugs. Dream on.

JM

ALSO BY J.M. LINK

ASKARI SERIES
SAVING ASKARA (TORI & ADERUS BOOK 1)
CHASING EARTH (TORI & ADERUS BOOK 2)
SPANNING WORLDS (MINA & JADAR)
FAE VEIL SERIES
WHEN FAE COLLIDE

AUDIOBOOKS
SAVING ASKARA, narrated by Keira Stevens
CHASING EARTH, narrated by Keira Stevens

`

Made in the USA
Las Vegas, NV
30 January 2021

16830189R00111